```
LP
WAT                              41006
                                 10-98


Watson, Clarissa


Somebody killed the messenger


TOWN HALL LIBRARY
P.O. BOX 158
NORTH LAKE, WI. 53064
```

SOMEBODY KILLED THE MESSENGER

A Persis Willum Mystery

CLARISSA WATSON

Thorndike Press • Thorndike, Maine

Library of Congress Cataloging in Publication Data:

Watson, Clarissa.
  Somebody killed the messenger: a Persis Willum mystery / Clarissa Watson.
    p. cm.
    ISBN 0-89621-867-8 (lg. print: alk. paper)
    1. Large type books. I. Title.
[PS3573.A848S6   1989]   89-30597
813'.54--dc19   CIP

Copyright © 1988 by Clarissa Watson.
All rights reserved.

Large Print edition available in North America by arrangement with Atheneum Publishers.

This is a work of fiction. Any references to historical events; to real people, living or dead; or to real locales are intended only to give the fiction a setting in historical reality. Other names, characters, and incidents either are the product of the author's imagination or are used fictitiously, and their resemblance, if any, to real-life counterparts is entirely coincidental.

Cover art by John Clarke.

For Alden,
who fulfills the need
of every author
for both a good lawyer
and an excellent son

SOMEBODY KILLED THE MESSENGER

Chapter 1

That day had begun routinely enough and progressed by the usual fits and starts until about two P.M., after which it deteriorated rapidly.

I remember the scene distinctly.

I had just returned from an exceedingly boring business lunch to which my employer, Gregor Olitsky, had dispatched me as a substitute for himself. A telephone was glued to his ear when I walked into his office.

His being on the telephone was not in itself particularly striking: the instrument was almost a part of his anatomy — his lifeline to the world.

What was striking was that he was back from lunch before I was: Gregor is a notorious gourmand who can barely persuade himself to rise from the luncheon table before dinner.

Nevertheless, there he was. Then I saw the remains of a roast beef sandwich on his desk and realized that, coward that he is, he had been hiding cravenly in his office to be absolutely certain he wouldn't be trapped into joining my tiresome little group after all. Gregor Olitsky will go to any extreme to avoid being bored, especially by artists keening about imagined mistreatment at his North Shore Galleries.

The minute he saw me, he rolled his eyes and made frantic gestures for me to pick up the other phone and when I did I understood his agitation — Seraphine Braceley was on the line. And we both knew that spelled trouble.

"I heard about the exhibition," she was saying as I tuned in, "and I want to know why I wasn't invited to send something. I have an important collection, too, in case you don't remember."

Everybody remembered. That was the problem.

I dug in my spurs and rode gallantly to the rescue. "It's Persis, Sera. How are you? How is your life of sin progressing?"

Seraphine and I are old friends and I can jolly her along like that. In fact, she rather likes to think of herself as some kind of scarlet woman, although by present-day standards she scarcely qualifies, having, as far as I know, taken up neither drugs nor kinky sex. All she does is marry people on a fairly regular basis.

"Persis. I suppose you mean by that, who am I married to these days?" She sounded neither more nor less excited than always, merely mildly displeased at having been interrupted just as she was getting started on

Gregor. "As a matter of fact, it's someone new — a lovely young Dutch antiques dealer named Frans Steen. Seraphine Steen . . . it reads well, don't you think? We're making it legal as soon as my divorce papers come through. Now, what about this show?"

I kept stalling. "This is a poor connection. Where are you calling from?"

As a matter of fact, the connection was perfect. But Gregor and I needed time to get ourselves together: the last thing we wanted now was an added starter to the Collectors' Choice show, particularly if it came from Seraphine.

"I'm calling from a restaurant in Amsterdam — the Tapperij Iijsbercht. It's dinnertime here. I tried to call you at breakfast but then I remembered the six-hour time difference and hung up."

So that was it. The telephone had nearly blown my head off at three A.M. I should have guessed.

"It's too late," Gregor protested. "Nothing you sent would get here in time. The preview is in four days."

"Never mind that. I have a messenger who will bring the painting by hand." She would be frowning, I knew, because she wasn't accustomed to opposition. She would also be a little drunk, probably on jenever since she was in

Amsterdam. Seraphine had always been polite about things like that. When in Rome . . .

I could even imagine exactly how she looked as she telephoned. Seraphine's looks were as memorable, it's safe to say, as her manners.

She was the youngest of six girls, each more statuesque than the one before. It was said that when her mother ushered them all into a club or restaurant, waiters would drop their trays at the vision of six Venuses in the flesh. Alfred Braceley, father of the brood, had persevered until he finally achieved a son — a sensible boy who was the antithesis of his sisters, all of whom looked like bawds who had just tumbled out of someone's bed, and probably had.

It was a look men (with the exception of poor Mr. Braceley) loved. And it had led to many marriages and divorces and newspaper stories among the sisters and, in Seraphine's case, to the outrageous and vulgar lawsuit that had almost got her drummed out of the social register. But not quite . . . her father was too rich for that to happen. In fact, it wasn't only the lawsuit that caused the trouble — although that was bad enough — but there was also the fact that a woman had died.

At that moment, if she was her usual self, Seraphine would be draped all over some unsuspecting man, and wearing extremely expensive clothes that she managed to make look as if she had rescued them from a Goodwill depot. Her Peter Paul Rubens body would be bursting every million-dollar seam. Her pale blond hair would be uncombed and unruly. And the man she was draped all over would probably be falling in love with her, although he wouldn't know it until too late.

That's how it was with the Braceley girls. No one ever understood it; but they were irresistible — at least in the beginning.

I wondered whom Seraphine was draped all over in that Amsterdam restaurant. Her new husband-to-be? Or someone she'd just met? She wasn't above marrying a casual acquaintance. Both the marrying and the drinking had begun after the lawsuit.

"Messenger?" Gregor was saying dubiously. "It's too late, Seraphine."

"Everything is done," I told her reasonably. "The invitations are out. The catalogues are printed...."

But she had no intention of listening to our objections. "Etienne and Sandro will be there, I suppose?"

Gregor looked as if he might faint. So I plunged gamely forward. "But naturally. You couldn't exclude them, could you? Their collections are too first-rate...."

Her voice dropped almost an octave and newly formed stalactites began to drip form every frigid syllable. "If that is the case, Persis, you and Gregor will include a painting from *my* collection as well. It will be brought by Dr. Pieter Joosten, who leaves tonight for Paris and will continue on Air France tomorrow for a conference at Harrington House in Gull Harbor. You may pick up the painting there any time after four. I promise you it will be worthy of your show. Dr. Joosten is a very distinguished scientist who's into new formulas like Brillat-Savarin was into rich recipes. You'll like him: he has beautiful pewter-colored hair." Trust Seraphine to be a keen observer of men's looks, even in times of crisis.

Gregor rallied bravely, as he is capable of doing when his back is truly to the wall. "Seraphine, you know perfectly well that it's insane to send a painting off like that. Your insurance people will have a fit. It's out of the question."

"Insurance?" I heard her laugh. "I haven't insured a painting in years. It's too expensive. And what's more, it won't cost a penny to send it this way. So don't be stupid."

There was a sudden terrific uproar on the Amsterdam end of the wire — loud voices, dishes clattering. I wondered if she had put the telephone down on the bar to kiss someone.

"Sera, Sera," I shouted. "You mustn't do this. It's out of the . . . we don't want . . ."

But she had hung up. Seraphine Braceley did not care to listen to objections. People who come from Gull Harbor are like that — imperious and spoiled. And Seraphine was no exception.

Gregor and I sat back and stared at one another.

Finally I said, "I suppose we ought to call her back."

"What good would that do?" Gregor answered. "She's been drinking. Our only hope is that she'll forget, or that the pewter-haired doctor will think better of serving as her messenger boy. After all, a painting makes a bulky package."

"But if he's traveling first class — and he's bound to be — they'll store it somewhere in the cabin for him. You and I have carried paintings back and forth dozens of times."

We sighed in unison. It had turned out to be one of those days. An added starter to the show was bad enough news at this late date. And any painting Seraphine would send . . . it didn't bear thinking about. Visions of irate collectors spun in our heads. Assaults on the gallery doors. Picketing. I struggled to find a bright side. "At least she didn't say she'd come in person, Gregor."

He shook his elegant head dolefully, staring down at where his shining Gucci shoes sank into the deep pile of his office carpeting. "I pray not — it would be a battle of the Titans."

We both paled a little, imagining the confrontation.

Now, Gregor Olitsky is many things besides being a world-class art dealer and gourmand. He is a millionaire, a ladykiller, and a formidable ballroom dancer.

But he is not, nor has he ever claimed to be, a soothsayer.

Nevertheless, he made a prediction. "We will live to regret this day," he pronounced, dabbing weakly at the permanent Palm-Beach tan of his unwrinkled brow with a hand-initialed Hermès handkerchief.

As it would turn out, he couldn't have been more right.

The armed guards stirred nervously and fingered their holstered handguns. There were three of them: they'd been on duty for two days, and this was the first sign of nervousness they'd betrayed.

I was staring at a Gauguin and wondering whether it or a blue-period Picasso should be featured in a certain spot, a decision that required all my concentration. So I barely noticed their agitation.

There were thirty paintings — most of them

already hanging, a few still lined up along the walls of Gregor Olitsky's North Shore Galleries waiting to be hung. Every one of them was a masterpiece, chosen as the favorites of their collections by thirty unimaginably rich Long Island collectors.

I had just decided to feature the Gauguin when I finally became aware of the kind of politely subdued commotion that would be noticeable only in a place as quiet as an art gallery.

It was exactly then that Withers, Gregor's tobacco-and-alcohol-wreathed personal secretary, ushered in two men.

My immediate reaction was that they were a far cry from the well-heeled types who ordinarily decorate a posh establishment like Gregor's. Gull Harbor, Long Island, where we all live and play and work, is the only place to be if you are both unimaginably rich and socially ambitious. It is populated by descendants of the original Four Hundred, all busily engaged in battling the creeping encroachment of "New Money," which they detest. (The only thing worse than having "New Money," is to have no money at all.) Consequently, people with new-minted fortunes haunt Gregor's gallery in search of the foolproof social prestige that comes from using their new money to buy old paintings, the older the painting and the bigger the price tag the better.

The two men Withers now presented were thin and shabby, with shadows of beard darkening their jaws, although it was barely ten-thirty A.M.

I had a wild impulse to call the Gull Harbor police to verify that they were who Withers, who never erred, said they were. But a long look at their greasy I.D.'s made me jettison the notion: they were genuine detectives, all right.

"What can I do for you, gentlemen?"

They were probably collecting for something. People usually were. The number of solicitors crossing the gallery's threshold every day appealing for worthy causes was positively terrifying. I couldn't understand how any business survived in Gull Harbor. Gregor was an exception: he was a millionaire. And even he did a lot of groaning.

But they weren't collecting for anything. Not today. "Persis Willum?"

I confessed that I was.

"Do you know a Dr. Pieter Joosten?"

"No." Technically true.

"A Seraphine Braceley?"

That was different. And ominous. "Of course. Why?"

"You telephoned Joosten several times on

the fourteenth." They weren't asking; they were telling me.

"Three times. The day he arrived. Any reason why I shouldn't?" Gregor had taught me always to try to answer one puzzling question with another.

"And three times yesterday, on the fifteenth. Six calls in all. Leaving messages to phone you at several different numbers."

"It was a busy day. I was moving around a lot, and I was anxious to speak to him."

They went on as if I hadn't spoken. "You said you were calling at Braceley's request."

"I was." Where was Gregor, I wondered? Where was he always when I needed him? Elsewhere, naturally. Having a massage or talking with his broker or still in bed after a gala night in town. Anyway, not here. Not when I could use his presence for the morale I needed every time they mentioned Seraphine's name.

What had she gotten us into?

"If you don't know Dr. Joosten, why were you telephoning him?"

"Business. He was bringing us a painting."

They looked taken aback. Their eyes met and gleamed briefly, like headlights signaling in the dark.

"Mrs. Braceley's — she phoned four days ago saying she wanted it to get here in time for the exhibition," I went on. "When Dr. Joosten didn't answer my calls, I assumed the painting hadn't come." And I'd heaved a sigh of relief. But I didn't add that.

They seemed to stretch toward me without actually moving, like hunting dogs on point. "What painting are we talking about?" Their eyes swept the masterworks in the room. All had big temporary labels still taped to them. Delacroix. El Greco. Bellini. Van Gogh. And the two shabby-looking men showed they weren't so shabby after all. "She must have been sending something important. What was it?"

"I don't know."

They didn't try to hide their disbelief: cynicism dripped from every pore like sap from a cut vine. "Could you say that again?"

I felt like a fool. "She didn't tell us. Is it important?"

"It could be."

I had a strong urge to sit down. "Would you gentlemen care to . . . ?" They wouldn't. But I did. And the next second I was glad I had.

They pointed to the morning's *New York Times* on a chair, still folded and unread. "You haven't seen the papers yet?"

"No."

They stared at me impassively. I must have been very pale. I know I felt that way. "You say that Dr. Joosten was bringing you a painting, but you don't know what it was?"

I nodded. There didn't seem to be anything to say. "Well, Mrs. Willum, Dr. Pieter Joosten has disappeared." I remembered what Gregor had said after Seraphine's call. "Oh, no."

"It's all in the paper. He checked into the conference center on schedule and registered without making an impression on anybody — it was a busy time. Apparently went to his room — went out again. Didn't turn up for the seminar he was supposed to attend. Bed not slept in. And so on. But it wasn't until some fishermen spotted his rental car under sixteen feet of water just beyond the Gull Harbor bridge that we were notified. Car windows and trunk were open. But no Dr. Joosten."

"It can't be. There must be some explanation. People don't just vanish."

"This one seems to have."

"And no painting?"

"No painting."

They asked more questions, which I answered mechanically. Mostly I think I said "yes" and "no." I remember asking what kind of scientist Joosten was supposed to be, and their saying he was a researcher in a number of fields, which for some reason surprised me.

Finally they left.

The door had scarcely closed when Gregor

appeared. He was waving yesterday's *Daily News* and all but foaming at the mouth. "That witch Francy James . . . Seraphine must have put her up to it. The terrible thing is that everybody — but everybody — reads her damn column. As you very well know, I am not averse to publicity. But this show is different. I'm striving for *dignity* . . . the hospital and all. We must project a dignified image when we're raising hospital money. Illness. Death. Pain. We must not have a breath of scandal. It's a whole different ballgame with hospitals. That witch!"

I tried to still the waters. "Calm down, Gregor. What has she said that's so terrible?"

"Calm down? Calm down?" His face had flushed and his neat gray mustache was twitching in agitation. "Listen to this, if you please . . . 'A much-married American heiress with a well-known penchant for European husbands may be about to wreak sweet revenge on a couple of famous names when an explosive painting, subject of a much-gossiped-about lawsuit, is unveiled as a surprise added starter in a charity benefit at a chic Long Island gallery this weekend.'"

"If nothing else," I said, striving for a neutral note, "she is mistress of the long-winded sentence."

"Damn it, Persis," Gregor roared, "this is

not the time for levity. This is serious."

I knew he was right. Two seedy-looking detectives were living proof that he was.

"She sent *the* painting," said my employer in notes of sheer despair. "The silly woman sent it. She's trouble . . . everything she touches turns to ashes. I wish I'd never heard of her."

"Gregor . . . you must calm down. It's not hers — how could she have sent it? Anyway, it didn't arrive — it's not here. It's gone."

He didn't seem to hear me. "I'll make her publish a retraction."

I went right on with what was really important. "There were two detectives here just now. Dr. Joosten's disappeared."

This time he paid attention. He grew very still and all the fire drained out of him. "It's begun, hasn't it?" he said. "Just as I predicted."

I went over and put my head on his shoulder. He felt warm and invincible and entirely safe. But I knew better. I knew that my beloved employer was the most fallible of men, prone to every human weakness. Much as I loved him, I could spend a whole day listing his frailties. Egotistical. Selfish. Superficial. A first-class sybarite. The kind who would be giddily fiddling while Rome burned.

But he had definitely, unquestionably, been

right the day the telephone call came from Amsterdam.

Lily Armbruster was the first to arrive at the preview. She came even before the doors were officially open. I heard the tap-tapping of the walking stick that heralded her arrival and looked desperately for a way to vanish into thin air. There was none. The curtain had gone up.

I suppose Lily had once been a beauty. She must have had something to capture a tough old tycoon like Abner Armbruster. But the vision making its way toward me showed no traces of its former glory.

Gregor had rushed forward and was bobbing and weaving along at her side. I knew he was praying he would get the old dragon out of the gallery before she could cheat him out of a painting. She had a history of helping herself to anything she fancied. Shopkeepers locked their doors and fled at her approach. Many had gone bankrupt because of her favors. When she paid at all, she paid her bills only once a year, and then had her lawyers settle for pennies on the dollar.

"I have come early to see that you have hung my Renoir in a proper light. The Met always hangs it in the dark, and that I will not tolerate."

I happened to know that the Met had *never*

hung her Renoir — rather, the late Abner Armbruster's Renoir. They always chose my aunt's instead.

"It's in the very best spot in the gallery for that particular Renoir," Gregor assured her. "Don't you agree, Persis?"

"I certainly do." As a matter of fact, I'd tried it in about ten different places in anticipation of this very moment. Too bad Aunt Lydie no longer lent her paintings — her Renoir was vastly superior. "I'm sure you agree, Mrs. Armbruster."

She wasn't at all certain that she did. The fact that it was glowing with color and that every flesh tone was shimmering didn't impress her. "I don't know. Perhaps over there. . . ."

She made dabbing motions at her thinning hair, which was dyed an alarming black. Her scalp peeked through here and there, delicate and pink as a baby's. Faux ringlets and curls had been pinned on in a dashingly random fashion, held precariously in place by an assortment of jeweled combs that glittered with a small fortune in diamonds and rubies. My heart bled for whatever jeweler she'd liberated them from. Ditto the diamond necklace and bracelets. One could only hope that these were tokens of Mr. Armbruster's passion for her, and not of hers for precious stones she had no intention of paying for.

Sometimes people wondered why nobody ever sued Lily Armbruster. But the old guard knew why. Minor lawsuits filled the Gull Harbor air like gnats on a summer day; but the rule was never, never to sue over anything that might make the front pages of the newspapers and thus cause a scandal. Like the Seraphine Braceley affair.

After a long discussion, Lily decided the Renoir looked all right. Then she pronounced the dread words. "Perhaps you'd like to show me what treasures you have hidden in your office, Gregor?"

Gregor leapt like a shot stag. "No, no, Lily — there's nothing good enough for you. Really. So let me give you a personal tour of the exhibition before the crowd comes in. Look at this. It's from Etienne Dehorter's collection. And over here is a picture Sandy Corsini traded with Picasso shortly before he died. Picasso loved Sandy's work, you know."

She snorted — an ancient goat that still had some flame. "Disgusting men, both of them. Trading that fool Seraphine whatever-her-name-is back and forth like a sausage. All that sex and scandal. If you have *that* picture here I shall withdraw my Renoir right now."

People were beginning to arrive, the men in black tie, the women done up as if they expected to meet at least a king or queen.

Gregor was frantic: he couldn't have Lily Armbruster making a scene.

"No, no, Lily," he said piously, "there won't be anything upsetting in this show. I guarantee it." He could, too — because he knew the painting had disappeared.

Lily Armbruster gave the twenty-nine other masterpieces in the room a cursory once-over. "Second rate," she pronounced loudly. Luckily the room was half full; the hum of conversation had begun. No one heard her.

Gregor and I drifted off to greet the guests, who were coming in like a stampede now, and Gregor was catlike with content: his fund-raising effort was going to be more successful than even he had anticipated. Gregor always said he couldn't tolerate semi-successes, and I always asked how he knew? — he'd never had a semi-success . . . all his successes were BIG, BIGGER, BIGGEST.

The gallery was getting crowded. People were jammed in shoulder to shoulder and I thanked heaven that the air-conditioning system hadn't broken down.

The lenders to the exhibition were a formidable group of movers and shakers in the financial and social world. New or old, they were all names that generated respect.

This evening was a two-thousand-dollar-ahead preview that would benefit Gregor Olitsky's second favorite charity, the Gull Harbor hospital. Gregor was raising funds because he wanted to be certain the hospital had the latest in everything, in case he ever had to go there.

His first favorite charity, naturally, was Gregor himself. He'd be the first to say so.

The list of collectors in the printed catalogue everyone was clutching was absolutely twenty-four karat, a cleverly balanced mix of old Gull Harbor gentry and nouveau riche, with a slight emphasis on the latter, since they were the ones who kept Gregor in business.

Lily Armbruster, for example, was among the oldest (and fiercest) of the Old Guard.

Randall McCoy had recently outbid the Japanese for a great Van Gogh.

Jordan Braceley, Seraphine's brother, had just bought an entire top collection of "Masters" European drawings.

Townsend Smith had inherited a magnificent Italian Renaissance collection from his mother.

Howard Roth and Simon Wheeler had agents scouring the world art markets for their collections.

Etienne Dehorter had donated his first collection to the Waldheim Museum and was building a second one based on the Expressionists.

Sandro Corsini, who'd been at the root of the scandal, had the most eclectic collection of all. A famous artist himself, he'd had the wit to trade his own work with the greatest artists of the twentieth century, often just before they died.

And so it went. Supported by new money or old, the collections were uniformly first rate.

And now they were all streaming in, collectors whose Gull Harbor houses looked like museums. And with them came the glitterati and their hangers-on. Limousines were pulling up in a line that stretched half a mile. Flash bulbs were lighting up the night, recording important entrances.

It was the most unbelievable timing. You might be tempted to believe Seraphine Braceley had been hiding in the bushes herself, waiting to give the signal.

Etienne Dehorter had just made his entrance, glamour oozing out around him in a halo. Actually, he looked godlike, with the aura of an aging but very splendid Apollo. He was undoubtedly at least seventy-five, but he still had the fit, youthful sheen that comes with being very rich. He even still had a full head of hair.

Hot on his heels came Sandro Corsini, a

study in contrasts if there ever was one. Short and peasant-stocky. Bald as a babe in arms. Stuffed into evening clothes that could have been borrowed from a trash basket. And exuding sexual prowess from every pore.

The two would not speak, of course, nor acknowledge the other's presence by so much as a glance. The drill would be for each to make a dash for the masterpiece he'd lent and stand there, chatting with admirers, until the evening was over.

But that's not how the script went tonight.

They had barely come in the door when two men in jumpsuits with Air France on the pocket came in, too. They were carrying a large package.

The armed guards leapt to attention. Gregor dashed forward.

"Package for Mr. Olitsky."

"I'm Olitsky."

"Sign here, please. This package was left unclaimed in the first-class cabin of a Paris–New York flight on the fourteenth. There was no sender's address, only yours. So we have delivered it to the address on the label."

I could see what looked like Seraphine's childish scrawl, handwriting that was practically illegible.

The gallery was in an uproar. Everyone had rushed up to cluster around Gregor. "How exciting . . . do open it up." I wondered if they'd all read James's column.

"Please, Gregor," I warned. "Open it in private."

"Don't be silly, Persis. How can I sign for something I haven't seen?" The crowd's excitement had infected him. Gregor adored electrifying incidents and this promised to be one of them. He began to tear at the wrappings.

I couldn't bear to watch. "Don't, Gregor — not here. Please don't."

But he was unstoppable now, his color high, his eyes burning with a kind of heedless blood lust I'd learned to recognize and fear.

It meant that the actor in him — never very far below the surface — had been aroused. He was playing to the audience, working for their attention and applause. At that moment Gregor Olitsky had a vision of himself onstage starring in his own drama, and wild horses couldn't have dragged him away.

What frightened me was that I suspected it was a drama Seraphine Braceley had written and directed and was planning to star in herself.

There was a sound of paper tearing. The wrappings fell away and the painting was revealed.

There was a gasp from the crowd.

"Let me see, let me see," howled *Newsday*'s

most ferocious art critic, plowing forward, long print skirt swirling against lean shanks.

"Oh, *mon Dieu,*" cried *Figaro*'s Arnaud Picard, tearing at his thinning hair in an effort to express his ecstasy.

Newsmen and newswomen we'd never seen before suddenly materialized and jostled collectors and guests to get near the painting. Dailies battled weeklies; TV battled radio. It was bedlam.

I looked around for Dehorter and Corsini. Naturally, they had vanished. One glance was all they'd needed.

Gregor had found an easel and was reverently placing the painting on it. All his former thoughts of Dignity, Illness, Death, Pain, and No Breath of Scandal had vanished in the red-hot fever of the moment. All he could see were tomorrow's headlines that were going to generate added revenues that would drop like manna from heaven into the till that was supporting his second favorite charity.

She was a naked courtesan, stretched out on silken sheets. Beneath her was a silken shawl. Her weight rested on her right elbow. She gazed at us with complete indifference, even contempt.

"Manet's *Olympia,*" someone whispered.

The painting that had caused a scandal when it was first exhibited in Paris in 1865. The critics had raged against it. "The flesh tone is dirty," they'd cried. "Her face is stupid, her skin cadaverous." Insults had rained down on the artist like hail: visitors to the exhibition had tried to attack the canvas.

Manet's *Olympia*. Her white flesh leaped out from the dark background. A maidservant hovered nearby, offering a bouquet of flowers.

Olympia . . . almost. Except —

The subject was Seraphine Braceley, unmistakable in all her nudity.

In the lower right of the canvas was written: "After Manet's *Olympia.*"

And the signature, very clear, read "Sandro Corsini."

This was it, finally. Never before seen. Seraphine. A painting that had caused a bigger scandal than Édouard Manet ever dreamed of.

A painting that had already caused the death of one woman.

A painting we'd been told had never arrived.

Chapter 2

The Seraphine-Corsini-Manet had first crossed our horizon about ten years earlier. Maybe sneaked unseen across our horizon would be more accurate.

It was another of those art events I seem to be eternally a part of. Not surprising, in view of the fact that I work in an art gallery, am also a painter, the niece of a famous art collector, and serve as the token starving artist on our own Waldheim Museum board of trustees.

This time it was the museum — a big bash to honor Etienne Dehorter for giving the Waldheim both his Impressionist collection and the funds for a new wing to house it.

We were all gathered at Pinky Williams's house to participate in the sort of celebration that is one of the ways museums all over the world extract priceless treasures from egotistical collectors. The main event of the evening was to be the unveiling — finally — of Sandro Corsini's painting of Dehorter's wife, which would hang next to Dehorter's in the new wing. Sandy'd been working on it for two years; and the impatient collector had declared tonight the absolute deadline.

The press was forbidden — this was private. Tomorrow the press would have its own party at the museum, complete with champagne and architect's renderings. But tonight they were *personae non grata.*

Pinky Williams and his wife Mary were comparative newcomers to Gull Harbor and they were laying on this extravaganza to score points where they counted. Pinky knew all the right moves, and underwriting an evening like this was definitely one of them.

The Williams house was a kind of mad contemporary version of Fort Knox with picture windows. It probably also had as much money inside it as Fort Knox at this moment, for Pinky had rounded up every living soul who mattered in Gull Harbor and environs. He knew that the way to turn out the biggest names was to produce enough other big names and a good cause. Pinky had produced both. What he hadn't produced was good weather. It was coming down in torrents and the terraces that should have absorbed the overflow of guests were awash to the gunnels.

What made it worse was that those terraces, covered with ghostly white tarpaulins ready to be whisked off in case the rain ever stopped, were clearly visible through the plate glass to the crush of guests so jammed inside the house that most of the waiters had finally given up trying to serve drinks and retired to the kitchen to do some serious drinking on their own.

I was wedged into a minuscule space between a window and the back of a chintz-covered loveseat, clutching a mordant Kir and listening to Lily Armbruster and the McCoys making conversation with Simon Wheeler and his wife, Tinka.

Naturally, they were talking about Seraphine Dehorter. I was barely listening. I hate that kind of chatter; but there was no way to escape.

"What do you suppose he'll have done with her? She's almost too beautiful to paint. I wouldn't want to try."

"Well, you know Sandy. There isn't a woman on earth he can't catch."

"On canvas or in person?"

"Don't be catty, love."

"Well, everyone knows what a devil Sandy is. Didn't his wife commit suicide or something like that?"

"Buried underneath the veils of time. Long before we knew him. Could be just rumor. But it surely makes him more interesting."

"A very attractive man, no matter what any of you say." It was Tinka, the self-appointed defender of everything to do with Sandy Corsini.

Half aware of Tinka going on and on, I amused myself by studying the tycoons in the room and trying to remember where their power came from. It wasn't easy. Having so many important men together in one place was confusing — they shot off sparks like lightning and it was hard to remember who was what. Most of them owned companies in multiples, with tentacles reaching into every industry one way or another. They put their money wherever there was money to be made and often went over each other's tracks in the process. Electronics, rocketry, medical research, banking — they were in it all. To a man they had warm smiles and cold eyes and probably hearts to match. Their wives, too. I suspected that not one of them would hesitate to hire a hit man if the situation warranted such extremes. That's how it is in Gull Harbor.

But the best thing was that I'd be seeing my old friend Seraphine. She'd be there for the unveiling of Sandy Corsini's painting, commissioned and paid for by the trustees as the final incentive to make Dehorter part with his collection. Sandy was the hottest young Surrealist (you must remember that Gull Harbor is conservative in the extreme) in the field. Everybody was scrambling to buy his dreamy paintings of empty-eyed people walking through strange ruins and deserted moonscapes.

And, as usual, he was keeping everyone waiting. It was part of his act.

"Can't wait to see what he's done with Seraphine," someone repeated. Whoever it was sounded jealous.

I spotted Howard Roth and his wife jammed into another section of the room talking to Samantha Swann, the magazine publisher, who was here tonight in her social persona, not as a journalist. They were all smiling toothily to prove there were no hard feelings because the Dehorters and not they were being celebrated. They, too, were probably jealous.

Jordan Braceley, all golden like his sister, was bent solicitously over the slightly shopworn but very uppercrust former debutante his mother was hoping he'd manage to marry. Her name was Missy, and she always looked as if something displeased her, which it probably did. Tonight that something was probably Seraphine's role as star of the evening. She would be jealous, too.

I couldn't see Henrietta and Alfred Braceley, Seraphine's parents, in the crowd, but they would certainly be there. Henrietta would rather be dead than miss all this.

Nor did I see Seraphine and Dehorter. Perhaps they were trapped in a different room. I missed Seraphine . . . since her marriage a decade ago I'd had only glimpses of her, mostly in the newspapers and glossy magazines as she followed her rich husband from spa to spa and benefit to benefit.

I did see Christine Kelley, the female jockey who had captured the press with her good looks as she rode successful race after successful race at Belmont and Aqueduct. Every win was big news. And every spill made sports-page headlines. Since she was a sort of female sports celebrity, she'd managed to breach the sacred walls of Gull Harbor and was now engaged in a ruthless hunt for the richest man she could land.

Marianna McCoy was looking daggers at her and I deduced that her husband, Randall, was the intended prey of the evening.

Lots of luck, Christine, I thought — I'd sooner tangle with a tarantula's mate than with Marianna McCoy.

Everyone was getting nervous by now. The drinks weren't flowing fast enough and people like the ones at this event have a very short attention span. They are easily bored; and their boredom ran like a wave across the room.

Ten more minutes, I thought, and they'll all bolt. Sandy had better turn up soon.

Townsend Smith read my mind. "If Corsini

doesn't get here in the next few minutes, this crowd will move to greener pastures. They're not used to standing around waiting for anyone."

"Let's go on to the club — at least we can get a drink there."

"No, no — let's wait five minutes more. You know Sandy — he's probably still painting the picture. Or setting it up downstairs in just the right light. He's such a perfectionist."

"Five minutes — and that's it."

They all agreed.

"I'm not interested in seeing a painting of her anyway," Tinka said. "It will only make me feel awful. She's too beautiful."

"Amen."

"And that's exactly the trouble," someone whispered. "She's too beautiful. It could be a curse."

"And amen to that, too," they all said in unison. "There's such a thing as too much of anything."

I'd never have thought there could be such a thing as too much beauty, but they were right, of course. They usually, in their mixed-up way, were. Even about the curse, although at the time it seemed absurd.

Chapter 3

I suppose she was. Too beautiful, I mean. That was the root of it all.

I was used to her looks by now. We'd been schoolgirls together at Greenvalley.

I knew all about her, too. And about her family . . . and especially about Henrietta.

I knew that her father was an Irish bricklayer named O'Braceley who became rich in construction and married a Presbyterian schoolteacher with social ambitions. The schoolteacher, Henrietta, had given him six ravishing daughters in a row before presenting him with a son.

When the first five girls married disastrously (according to Henrietta's precepts), Seraphine had been wangled into the upper-crust sanctuary of Greenvalley by Mr. O'Braceley's writing of huge tax-deductible checks. The *O* had been stricken from the O'Braceley name, the family had turned Episcopalian, and Seraphine had walked into my life.

Henrietta Braceley had been from birth a

woman of definite ideas about what was socially acceptable and what was not. My aunt, Lydia Wentworth, used to say that Henrietta Braceley slept with the Stud Book beneath her pillow. And by that she didn't mean the record of thoroughbred horse sires and dams, but the black book with the red lettering on it known formally as the *Social Register,* which purported to list the same kind of breeding in humans. Aunt Lydie and everyone she knew had long since had themselves removed from it, but to the nouveau riche, it was a kind of bible — holier, even.

Seraphine may not have been born into the Stud Book, but she was born beautiful in a completely and mysteriously grown-up way. And Henrietta Braceley, figuring that Seraphine was her last bankable treasure — her last chance to break into what she thought of as Society — had negotiated her youngest daughter's enrollment in Greenvalley and dedicated her life to augmenting that education through long, exhaustively instructive letters on how to get ahead in the world.

Now, I would never say that Seraphine Braceley was stupid: rather she was lazy and uninterested in education, having been drilled from birth to expect to marry a millionaire and spend the rest of her days doing nothing more intellectually demanding than instructing servants in their chores.

But she did pay meticulous attention to Henrietta's daily letters and she really tried to absorb their commands, which were often relayed — as if the word of God — to me.

"Gentlemen don't play golf," Henrietta once wrote, "although a place like Gull Harbor might be excepted. A gentleman's sports are hunting, shooting, and sailing. The only proper 'ball' sports are tennis, polo, and squash. For a grown man to spend a whole day pursuing a golf ball is bizarre and, worse yet, plebeian."

On another occasion she wrote, "Gentlemen are not expected to be educated except in business and sports. They are not required to speak other languages or to know more about music than the titles of a few key operas. They must, however, know about wines."

Seraphine was an obedient child: she read every word and, in fact, kept the letters in a packet, which she frequently reread when she should have been studying.

On second thought, maybe she was studying.

She certainly never gave any encouragement to the hordes of young men who pursued her: they simply didn't measure up to Henrietta's standards. "I'll know the right one when I meet him," Seraphine would say. And my money was on her and on Henrietta's scriptures, because Henrietta Braceley knew that what the family needed was not money — there was plenty of that — but a marriage so brilliant it would wipe out the older sisters' famous failures and establish the Braceleys once and for all in Gull Harbor society.

I honestly don't think Seraphine cared a rap about any of this. But she knew her duty. No "inappropriate" young man would lay a hand on her. She would make friends with rich girls at Greenvalley. Through them, she would meet their socially impeccable brothers, none of whom, it was correctly assumed, would be able to resist her. From among these she would choose the most appropriately eligible.

The Braceleys sat back confidently to await the results.

For years the flow of letters remained uninterrupted, forming a sort of back-up education to the one Greenvalley was striving to give her. For years Seraphine stretched, yawned, submitted cheerfully to school routine and sports, and absorbed practically nothing. It was by informally tutoring her through one scholastic crisis after another that I got to know her so well and became so fond of her.

"Help me, Persis. If I flunk, my parents will die."

So I did and they didn't.

You couldn't help liking her. Even those girls who were jealous of her beauty couldn't resist her careless charm. She didn't seem to be interested in any of the usual schoolgirl things: clothes, boys, or how she looked. She didn't have to — she looked great in anything, the boys swarmed around her like demented bees, and she was always gorgeous, even when she first got up in the morning and should have been a mess.

And always Henrietta Braceley reminded her, "It's just as easy to fall in love with a very *rich* society man as with a poor one": Henrietta was eminently pragmatic.

I suspect that Etienne Dehorter arrived just in time. Seraphine was ripe for the plucking.

I was there when it happened.

We were at a polo match at the Gull Harbor club. After the game the players stopped for a drink at the clubhouse.

It was Etienne Dehorter's debut in Gull Harbor. His parents were French. He'd been educated at Eton; and his Frenchness combined with his Englishness gave him an air of almost unbearable Continental elegance. ("God," Henrietta had once instructed in a letter, "is, as you know, an Englishman; and his greatest creation is the English gentleman." Seraphine knew at once that she was meeting God's greatest creation.)

If I'd often wondered what elements defined the English gentleman, Henrietta's daily letters provided the answer: "The true gentleman," she said, "can wear shirts frayed at the collar as long as his suit comes from Savile Row and his shoes are handmade."

On another occasion she wrote, "Panama hats are the true test: they must have a ridge down the center instead of a dent."

After that Seraphine and I spent weeks searching for a gentleman in a Panama hat, but we never found one.

All of these pronouncements were nothing compared to the letter in which Henrietta instructed her daughter on the niceties of the proper weekend. "Remember," she wrote severely, "that no gentleman arrives for the weekend with a brand-new gun case and always in a button-down collar under a sweater. He *never* goes shooting in a jacket with leather on it. He *never* wears synthetic fabrics. But if he comes for the weekend with a leather collar box, it is a good sign."

Good sign or no, since men weren't allowed to spend weekends at Greenvalley, this information, though interesting, was not much use to Seraphine.

Until Dehorter.

Because as soon as he changed from his polo kit to civilian gear she discovered that he had all the right credentials — frayed collar, hand-made shoes, wool sweater, and all.

He even, she confided after she'd known him a few weeks, had an ivory-handled toothbrush. I forbore to ask her how she knew this, although I would have staked my life that it wasn't knowledge acquired first hand: Seraphine was still, in those days, truly innocent. Doubtless it was one of her mother's tests of a gentleman, and Seraphine must have asked him.

They fell in love at once, and cannons went off all over Gull Harbor — probably on the Continent as well. The most eligible bachelor was marrying the most beautiful girl, with scarcely a pause to get to know one another.

She was just seventeen.

He was a perfectly preserved and debonair fifty-five.

Chapter 4

"Have you seen Seraphine and Etienne?" It was Pinky, nervous and perspiring. Somehow he'd managed to wade his way through the mob and reach us.

"No sign of them in this room," Tinka answered. "Maybe they've had a fight or something. Persis, do you think she's ever regretted marrying such an older man?"

I'd wondered about that, myself. I'd even tried half-heartedly to warn her in the beginning. Dehorter had never been married before. He was an international, much-pursued bachelor when she met him. Nearly forty years older. Set in his ways. Accustomed to adulation and flattery. Seraphine was his first adventure in matrimony. For all I knew he may have considered her just one more beautiful acquisition for his art collection. Certainly I'd never seen him hold hands with her or heard him call her sweet names or do any of the things people expect of a man finally smitten by love. If he was a lover, he was a very reserved and formal one.

As for Seraphine, she was such a brainwashed, wide-eyed, indolent innocent that I doubt she even thought beyond the wedding. Dehorter measured up to every one of her mother's requirements: ergo, they would live happily ever after. Isn't that what Henrietta's letters had always promised?

So I looked Tinka straight in the eye. "I haven't seen Seraphine in several years, you know. But I'm sure she's very happy."

"I wouldn't bet on it," Wheeler said.

I thought about the slight downturn to her perfect mouth that had showed up in recent photographs. But maybe it was my imagination. My own marriage had been a disaster: maybe I was suffering from an attack of sour grapes. It was ten years since the wedding, and they were still together.

They were talking about Sandy now.

". . . late, of course. Always is. Part of the act." That was Pinky, rather cross.

". . . women mad for him . . . know for a fact . . ." Randy McCoy joined the conversation.

". . . gorgeous man . . . absolute winner . . ." That was the magazine publisher, Samantha Swann, who had managed to squeeze into our circle.

Through the door to my left I could see several steps down into the large yellow and white drawing room which teemed with people. If I really craned my neck I could look the other way into a hall where several brave and desperate men were inching their way through the solidly packed bodies toward what they hoped would be a bar. A quick mental calculation told me that it would take fifteen minutes each way, not counting time out for conversations en route.

I wondered briefly if it would be worth it to struggle into the drawing room to talk to some new faces, and decided it wouldn't. Then I tried to imagine what someone from outer space would think if he landed in the middle of this party.

I gazed into the night; the rain had let up a little. From previous visits I knew that the house sat atop a hill without another house in sight, and that far below, silver in its tree-lined setting and just visible now, there was a small lake about the size of a football field.

A flicker of light caught my eye. I watched idly, waiting for it to reappear, wondering what it was. My eyes became better adjusted to the dark and I saw another flicker. Then out it came from between the trees, chugging along in a more or less straight line like a faithful, industrious beetle, very small and very steady, right to the edge of the lake and in. Kerplonk.

For a stunned second or two I stared, half

expecting it to bob to the surface and swim away. But it didn't.

I looked around. There should have been screams or cries of shock. But there weren't — everyone was carrying on exactly as before, and somebody was even handing me his card and mumbling about lunch. I gave the lake one more look to be sure it really existed. It existed all right.

That's when I did the thing that made Pinky so mad, even though he knew I had to, because it ruined the evening.

There was a little white telephone on a table practically underneath my right hand. I picked it up and dialed the number every Gull Harborite has memorized in case of need.

"Police?" I told them where I was calling from. "I think you'd better come and take a look at this lake down here. Something — a golf cart or power mower, I'm not quite sure what — just drove into the water and never came out. And I think there was somebody on it."

Chapter 5

It would turn out to be a seven-day wonder, the finding of the Body on the Power Mower, but nothing more than that. It didn't really seem to have anything to do with anything that was going on that night except that I saw it happen. The mower came from Pinky's toolhouse, and the dead woman was a part-time reporter or "stringer" for Samantha Swann.

The police came and took statements and thoroughly wrecked Pinky's party. They dredged the power mower and its passenger out of the lake (which turned out to be very shallow). They snooped all over the grounds, flashlights flickering like furious fireflies. And they finally went away.

Sam Swann is very protective of the collection of has-beens that work for her. Her admiration for writers — even those whiskey-soaked beyond redemption — has remained unshaken through years of missed deadlines, garbled facts, and maddening misspellings. When she learned that it was one of her "staff writers" who had perished in the lake, she rushed off to headline the event in her next month's issue.

"Famed *Posh* (that's the name of her magazine) Correspondent Dies — Is It Murder?" she wrote in large black type. "Newswoman Felled By Blow While Riding Power Mower" her subhead continued, clearly implying that there had been foul play; although by the time the magazine came out the inquest had established, for lack of evidence, that it was a case of accidental death, a verdict Sam clearly challenged. Why would her reporter be skulking about in the rain on a power mower, she demanded to know? Surely not to get details of Pinky's party — Samantha herself was *there*. And a blow on the head from a falling branch (there were a lot of them around after the storm) — nonsense. It was plain as a pikestaff, she wrote, that the poor woman had been struck on the head, loaded aboard the stolen mower, and pointed in the direction of the lake with the certain knowledge that the machine would go unswervingly into it and drown its burden. She had climbed aboard the mower herself with her photographer standing by, pointed it toward the lake, closed her eyes, and proved her point, more or less. The police, she insisted, must keep the case open.

The police smiled and held their counsel.

They knew that the Famous Correspondent was:

a. A hopeless alcoholic;

b. Also a stringer for columnist Francy James's New York column and that, unlike the very social Sam Swann, Francy James hadn't been invited to Pinky's bash;

c. And light-fingered to boot. They suggested delicately to Pinky that he check his inventory, because the Famous Correspondent's lust for liquor was such that if the power mower was the only thing missing, Pinky was damn lucky.

In a few days the Famous Correspondent was buried and forgotten by everyone except her landlady, the local barkeep, and others to whom she owed money. Even Sam Swann surrendered when people began banging on her door, hoping she'd pay off the F.C.'s debts.

And it was only then that Gull Harbor woke up and discovered that a real Class-A Gull Harbor-type scandal had been taking place right under its nose while all eyes were glued on the power mower and the lake.

I remember exactly what I was saying to someone when Pinky came to get me. "I'll bet it was parked at the side of the house, waiting to be used to pull away the tarpaulins if the rain stopped. She didn't want to ruin her shoes, so she climbed up. . . ."

The party was a shambles. Everyone was fighting to get to his car and get home.

And Pinky, without success, was trying to stop them.

"The presentation — you can't leave. Sandy has arrived. We're unveiling the picture. Please . . ."

All of which proved that Pinky hadn't assimilated into Gull Harbor. If he had, he'd have known that the mere arrival of the law meant his party was over. Gull Harbor doesn't tolerate uncouth situations; and the presence of police came under the heading of an uncouth situation to be avoided at all costs. They were swarming overboard like proverbial rats leaving the proverbial sinking ship.

But Pinky hadn't yet acquired the savoir-faire to realize that once the police were aboard, his ship was definitely sunk.

"Sandy's here," he cried, clutching my arm.

Wouldn't you know, I thought, that Sandy would finally arrive right in the middle of a disaster? Like the typical vague artist, he had probably wandered in with his assistant and his painting and never even noticed that something else was going on. Maybe he thought all those flashing lights were for *him*. Sandy, after all, was used to being a star.

"Where is he, Pinky?"

"Downstairs in the library. Oh, this is awful.

The museum staff are waiting but I can't find anyone else. Everyone's left."

"Never mind. I'll round up a couple of trustees and be down. There must be somebody around."

But there wasn't, and anybody who was still there was interested only in getting out.

So I went down by myself. And when I saw the tableau that greeted me outside the library door, I was glad. Sandy was lying on the floor, blood running down his face from a cut on his forehead. Dehorter was standing over him with a poker, screaming. Sandy's "assistant," a youth of about thirteen, was trying to pull the enraged Dehorter away from the fallen artist. Everyone else — museum staff and Seraphine too — was backed up against the wall of the corridor, pale with terror.

Pinky and I joined the fray, falling upon Dehorter and dragging him back before he could inflict further damage. Dehorter was quite beside himself. "I'll kill you if you don't get that picture out of here. No one is to see it — you understand? No one goes into that room until it's gone. All of you people — out. This minute!"

The museum staff took to their heels and fled, eyes rolling in fear. Violence doesn't usually roil the academic waters: they weren't prepared to cope, especially as the madman with the poker was their illustrious new patron.

Sandy's assistant managed to open the library door, drag his master inside, and lock it. Etienne leaned the poker carefully against the wall and offered Seraphine his arm.

"Tell Corsini that he will hear from my lawyers in the morning." He certainly would.

And so — figuratively speaking — would everyone else.

Chapter 6

The Battle of Agincourt couldn't have been much worse than the court battle that followed.

Everyone quickly dubbed our local war the Battle of the Waldheim, which didn't make the museum and its trustees very happy.

Dehorter sued Sandro Corsini for defamation of his wife's character, even though he could produce no painting nor even photographs to prove it.

The museum sued Corsini for breach of contract, claiming that the artist had not delivered a portrait of Dehorter's wife as commissioned.

Corsini countered by suing them both: Dehorter for assault and battery and the museum for breach of *his* contract, claiming in turn that he had never been commissioned to do a portrait per se but rather a serious painting using Dehorter's wife as a model, that he had delivered such a painting, that he had been promised public recognition at the unveiling and not received it, and that he had not been paid a penny for two years of hard work.

Sam Swann and everybody else had a field day with the story. The poor Famous Correspondent was rapidly shunted to the back pages and eventually out of the news altogether in favor of the more glamorous Seraphine and Etienne Dehorter, Sandy Corsini, and the Waldheim Museum. It was an Art Event made for headlines: Fracas Disrupts Museum Dedication... Society Beauty Incites Fisticuffs ... Embattled Museum Fights Famous Artist ... Husband Banishes Painting of Wife. And, of course, they all looked wonderful in their photographs, even when skulking in or out of court.

Dehorter hired a top law firm to handle his case. Corsini placed his affair in the hands of a lone warrior who immediately pointed out that his client's civil rights had been violated. The museum left it all to the trustees, who among them engaged another gaggle of law firms. Gull Harbor, which didn't approve of this kind of litigation, was nevertheless delighted with it all. They considered drumming Seraphine and Dehorter out of the social register, but thought better of it. After all, the two of them had furnished a season's amusement.

Eventually everyone settled out of court and undisclosed amounts of money changed hands.

While these unpleasantnesses were taking place, Henrietta Braceley displayed a surprisingly high profile. Surprising because I would have thought she'd have taken just the opposite tack.

It must have had to do with her son, Jordan, who was, I suppose, her last chance, the last remaining perfect golden arrow in her quiver. He was in a very vulnerable position just then vis-à-vis his future membership in several exclusive clubs that Henrietta considered imperative for a gentleman's pedigree, clubs that would guarantee the final finish needed to achieve the society marriage she planned for him.

From the beginning Henrietta chose quite coolly to be very visible and, by associating herself firmly with Dehorter, to deliberately diminish the impact of Seraphine's disgrace.

She took up a position at a rather reluctant Dehorter's side, clinging to his arm so possessively that I, for one, was hard-pressed to decide whether he was supporting her or if it was the other way around. Or whether this was a lawsuit or a royal funeral.

Seraphine was left to wander along on her

own while her mother made it clear that she and Dehorter were courageously facing the distasteful events together, united against the calumny that had been visited upon their fair names.

Henrietta even took to wearing a pearl choker and a brimmed hat with a dark veil. The comparison to the famous photograph of Britain's Queen Mary in mourning was duly noted by the press. With consummate skill, she managed to create the impression that she and Dehorter were distancing themselves behind some invisible barrier from the naughty child whose peccadilloes and indiscretions had sullied two family trees. In fact, Henrietta even persuaded her husband to make several appearances at Dehorter's side to give the impression that the two families were practically one; and that the unfortunate Seraphine's adventures had no more to do with them than those of England's often wayward princesses and princes had to do with the royal family itself. These things were simply something one must bear in such an exalted position in life.

Poor Braceleys. That's what everyone ended up saying.

Nobody thought about poor Seraphine.

Except me. I tried to call her to offer what comfort or help I could. But she responded to neither calls nor letters.

So I tried Henrietta.

"There must be something I can do," I told her.

"Nothing," was the cold response. "She's speaking to no one but the family, on my orders. Etienne quite agrees."

"But I'm her friend. Surely . . ."

"She's in seclusion. She's made enough trouble. I am only doing what is right. I am a lioness protecting my own."

By that did she mean she was protecting her own daughter, her own son-in-law, or her own family name, I wondered?

But I didn't argue. Nobody argued with Henrietta. She was, after all, the self-proclaimed authority on all codes of conduct and on almost everything else including, I was sure, lionesses and their duties.

Shortly before the settlement — and doubtless much to the relief of her mother and husband — Seraphine disappeared. Nothing was seen or heard of her. She could have vanished in smoke.

But two weeks later she reappeared. Apparently she had thought things over because she packed up her belongings, moved in with Corsini, and sued Dehorter for divorce. When the divorce was final, she married Sandy, lived with him for about a year, packed up again, left for Europe, and never returned.

Henrietta, who had already suffered enough, might well have taken to her bed and perished of chagrin. But she must have been inured to disappointment by her five earlier failures.

Henrietta definitely survived.

I wasn't so sure about Seraphine.

Now, eight years after leaving Corsini, she had a drinking problem, had gifted her mother with a fifth Seraphine-son-in-law, and was threatening to give her a sixth.

I would never have believed it.

Chapter 7

The Corsini-Seraphine-Manet *Olympia* gazed scornfully down at the crowd from its temporary perch on the big studio easel. The crowd milled around it, gasping with excitement. Gregor beamed beatifically on one and all.

Afterward, no two people agreed on the exact sequence of events, and the press got no real photos of the proceedings because the men of Gull Harbor, in full evening regalia, closed ranks, crowded between the photographers and the combatants, and obscured the fighters and the painting itself in a sea of black. It was an example of what's so marvelous about Gull Harbor — fiercely competitive though these men are, when there's a crisis it's "them" against "us" every time.

One thing we all did agree on — it was very nearly a rerun of their last meeting; Dehorter sprang upon Corsini, whose back was turned, and hurled him to the floor while startled cameramen tried to catch the image of an elegant millionaire perched like an animal on the back of one of America's most eminent artists.

All they ended up with was a shot of Seraphine's face and one bare painted breast.

It was quickly finished.

There was an embarrassing thrashing of bodies on the floor — an unheard of public display in an area where good manners are more important than good sex. And in due time one group of black-and-white clad gentlemen removed the combatants while another removed the painting to Gregor's office. That ended the evening.

It was hard for me to imagine that I could have lived through such a scene twice, but I did.

And I wondered if that was the way Seraphine had planned it. But no — Seraphine wasn't that clever. She wasn't clever at all.

That, at least, is what I kept telling myself. Perhaps it was wishful thinking. After all, I really didn't know her anymore.

Chapter 8

It took two days for Gregor to stop dog-paddling around in a sea of attention and thrills. The public was beating a path to his gallery door — many of them people who'd never before looked at a picture. Such is the power of the press.

On the third day he saw the light. Henrietta Braceley opened his eyes.

He summoned me to his office and poured two glasses of sherry. It was an ominous sign — he always served sherry when something was troubling him.

"Sit down, Persis. I want to talk to you."

I arranged myself obediently on one of his brown leather chairs and looked attentive.

"Have you succeeded in reaching Seraphine?"

I shook my head. "No. I started phoning everywhere the night of the preview and I haven't stopped since. No luck at all."

"And have you learned anything about that Dr. Joosten?"

Again I shook my head. "They say at the conference center that they were expecting him. He's a Dutch scientist who's done some interesting work in metallurgy, among other things . . . a sort of scientific jack of all trades, I gather. But not anything that would get him kidnapped or killed."

"Well, you'd better find out something. Those detectives have been in and out of here so many times I'm beginning to feel a certain fondness for them. But they don't exactly decorate the landscape, do they?"

I smiled. "They lend a certain air, I think. What about the painting? Wouldn't it be politic to remove it from the show? The rest of the collectors must be furious about all the notoriety."

"Tell me about it. God! The way they've dragged out that old scandal — the old photographs — the old lawsuits. It's horrible." But he didn't really think so; he was enjoying it all, still giddily, deliriously wallowing in the publicity.

For the last two days I'd been trying to keep my head in order to cope with the day-to-day business of the gallery, which was my responsibility. It hadn't been easy. And Gregor made it immediately clear that it wasn't going to get easier.

"Henrietta Braceley," he told me, "is threatening to take us to court if we don't remove Seraphine's picture from the show. And she means business, Persis."

"I imagine she does." No one who knew Henrietta could doubt it. "Then why don't you remove it?" Why hadn't he done it immediately? But of course I knew the answer to that — the publicity. And a bigger gate for his second favorite charity.

"I can't."

"Why on earth not?" It was his gallery and his show, after all.

"The police. They don't say so in so many words, but it's obvious we're suspected of having something to do with the vanishing Dr. Joosten. So it behooves us to cooperate with them. And they've requested that the painting remain in the show."

A vivid mental image flashed onto the often empty screen of my mind. It was full of faces of enraged collectors — collectors who provided Gregor's (and thus my) livelihood.

"Can they make you do that, Gregor?"

"I don't know. But cooperation is indicated. Except on the other hand there's the formidable Henrietta. I don't know who to fear most."

There was no question in my mind. "I think you should remove the painting. I never thought you should show it in the first place.

The sooner that painting is out of sight, the better."

It was so like Seraphine to do something dumb and then leave it to someone else to clean up the mess.

"Then find her," Gregor said.

I put down my sherry. "What?"

"Find her. Get her to explain to the police. Find out what happened to Joosten — she must know. Get us off the hook with everyone. The minute the police talk to her they'll let us remove the painting and that will get everyone off my back."

I stared at him, not believing what I had heard. "You can't be serious. If the police can't track her down. . . ."

"She's probably sleeping peacefully somewhere with somebody and doesn't even know that Joosten didn't arrive. She's probably gloating somewhere about the discomfort she's caused her two husbands and hasn't any idea that we're in trouble. Maybe she's hiding out so Dehorter and Corsini can't get even with her. But if she knows you're looking for her — you, her friend . . . She may be scared stiff by now at what she's done."

"They'll find her eventually," I told him.

The gray mustache twitched. "Who? The people who made off with Joosten? Suppose they killed him? Suppose she knows something about that? Suppose she was there when it happened?"

I laughed, but it was a weak laugh. "They say at the conference center that he never discovered anything important enough to be kidnapped."

"What if they're wrong? What if they track her down and . . ."

I rummaged in my mental appointment book to see if there was anything pressing I could offer as an excuse. A wild goose chase through Amsterdam wasn't high on the list of my priorities. But there was nothing. Not even anything mildly pressing.

"I'll pay your expenses, of course."

I knew what that meant: barely enough to cover one cheap meal a day and quarters in a third-rate hotel. "Well, thanks — but . . ."

The politely blinking light on Gregor's telephone console informed him that he had a call, but he made no effort to answer it. That's when I realized that matters were indeed serious. "The police say they want the painting left on display as bait — that's the word they used, although I'm not at all sure what they meant by it. Of course, I have to cooperate with the law — it would be unthinkable not to, no matter how unreasonable their request may seem. And Henrietta, on the other hand, will sue us for all we're worth if we don't remove it.

So you see, you have to find Seraphine — she's the only one who can resolve this problem."

He could be right. "One thing has been bothering me. The *Olympia* belonged to Sandy. Why doesn't he just take it and run?"

Gregor shook his neat gray head, stroked his equally neat mustache. "He's keeping out of it and implying to the police that he gave the painting to Seraphine while she was his wife. It could be true, although it's not his style to be so generous. Maybe he doesn't want the publicity, although that's not like him, either."

Gregor was right: the only time I'd known Sandy to give away one of his canvases was in exchange for the work of another artist whom he admired. He was a hard-bargaining businessman who had parlayed his talent into a fortune. Giving anything to anyone for free was not his style. Furthermore, he loved personal publicity of any kind. It didn't make sense that he hadn't snatched up the *Olympia* and run back to his studio with it.

"I don't understand any of it," I said gloomily.

"Nobody does. But if she's going to surface at all and explain, it will be to you. Go to that restaurant. Ask around. Amsterdam is a small place: somebody will tell her you're looking for her. See what you can do. I can stall

Henrietta for a couple of days, but that's all. Withers has your ticket."

It was all over but getting on the plane.

I trudged back into my office to clear my desk and make a few last phone calls. I kept remembering what he'd said about the police. They wanted the *Olympia* left on display — as bait.

But what were they hoping to catch? And mightn't it be dangerous?

And for whom?

No — it was absurd. I would find Seraphine — a woman that beautiful couldn't vanish without her absence being noted. Joosten, too, would turn up somewhere. The painting, which was, after all, an inanimate object and therefore harmless, would be taken from display. Henrietta would be mollified. The police would retire from the scene. And all would be right with the world.

Meanwhile, there was Amsterdam.

Chapter 9

When I enter the Dutch countryside by automobile, which is how I've usually arrived, I think of it as a dark green bowl filled to the brim with black-and-white cows. That's how it still looked coming in by air. From high above, the ribbon-thin channels of water dividing the lush pastures were like narrow silver frames around a painting.

The hotel Gregor had selected for me wasn't as bad as I had expected. It was named the Eureka and it was small and neat and on the Amstel River, within easy reach of everything. He'd probably noted it from the windows of one of the expensive hotels he frequented on the other side of the canal. At the moment it was filled with a visiting opera troupe, and occasional bursts of song echoed in its small lobby or from patrons clustered around the bar that stood just inside the front door.

My feelings about Amsterdam have always been ambivalent.

Naturally I love the museums. The Vermeers

at the Rijksmuseum are incomparable, and they alone are worth the trip — so are the Rembrandts. The Van Goghs, the moderns at the Stedelijk are nothing less than dazzling. I even love the great elaborate barrel organ stationed outside the Rijksmuseum cranking out jolly tunes.

I love the architecture — the tall, narrow houses, some of them leaning at precarious angles, the patterned brick, the gabled warehouses with their exposed pulleys, the beautiful parks, the mounted policemen in black leather on their proud, sturdy horses.

I love the small canals with their moored houseboats full of cats and books, and the leafy green elms that shelter them.

The permanence of this city, built on thousands of wood pilings because it is largely below sea level, never ceases to astonish me. Why hasn't it sunk into the sea? How does the railroad station stay above ground? How can rotted pilings ever be replaced?

But the Amsterdammers in their wisdom have worked it out somehow.

It is a near-perfectly planned city built around concentric canals: the Singelgracht, the Herengracht (the gentleman's canal), the Prinsengracht (the prince's canal), and the Keizersgracht (the emperor's canal).

And the citizens themselves are as astonishing

as their city. They are multilingual, orderly, and probably the most tolerant people in the world.

Perhaps they are too tolerant: Amsterdam is the European capital for hippies. Drugs are tolerated. So is sexual originality. Sex shops flourish. There are always beautiful girls on display in the ground floor windows of the zeedijk, the red-light district. The central square, the Dam, is filled with modern refugees from less tolerant countries. But Amsterdammers stick to their tradition of live and let live.

Everything is tolerated by the government. Everyone is tolerated. That's why I am ambivalent.

And it's probably why Seraphine had chosen to come here.

Perhaps Amsterdam had become the perfect city for her. Because from everything I knew, the Seraphine of today was different from the Seraphine I'd known.

I started out on foot after asking directions to the restaurant she'd phoned from the last time we heard from her. The hotel knew it well. "Everyone goes there," they said.

The Tapperij Iijsbercht was a pleasant-looking place on the Herengracht canal. The staff was getting ready for the luncheon rush when

I arrived. One waiter was washing down the sidewalk. Inside, a squad of white-aproned youths was laying tables and polishing glasses. A long bar ran down the length of the left side of the room and in the back a flight of steps led up to a balcony with tables already laid.

There were a few men at the bar. As it was not yet noon, I deduced that it is never too early to order a drink in Holland. They all turned and looked me over politely.

"Would you like to order an apéritif?" The barkeep spoke perfect English. Almost everyone I've ever met in Amsterdam does.

I looked quickly to see what the other customers were having. Whiskey, neat. I can't tolerate anything as strong as whiskey at any hour, let alone so early in the day. "Well . . ."

He came to my rescue. "Perhaps a jenever — a Dutch gin?"

What was it Seraphine always said? When in Rome . . . ?

"Jenever. Why not?"

"A small one — a *borreltje?* It's not too much."

"Fine." If the people in this restaurant were going to be of any help to me, I'd better show goodwill, even if it meant a hangover afterward. "I've never tasted jenever."

They all thought I was kidding, especially

the bartender. "In this city of a thousand bars? Well, you'll like it. American women all seem to like it. It's cheap and it's good."

He was big and he was hairy and he was delighted to have a woman at his bar. He poured the jenever with great ceremony into a small neat glass and served it to me with a bow and some kind of jovial-sounding toast in Dutch, which I couldn't understand. The other men raised their glasses to me in a gesture of goodwill and we all drank.

One of the men at the bar addressed me politely. He, too, spoke perfect English. Probably this ubiquitous fluency in her native tongue was another thing that had attracted Seraphine, who was no linguist, to Amsterdam.

"You must try a jenever with our famous raw herring and with a beer chaser," he told me.

I tried to keep smiling and not choke to death. After whiskey, two of the things I like least are herring and beer. Aunt Lydie says it's because I'm a snob but she's wrong — it's because they make me ill.

"Do American women also take herring and beer here?" I asked when I had recovered.

The barkeeper wrinkled his large fleshy nose disdainfully. "Most of them don't care for herring."

One of the regulars interceded, afraid I

might be offended. "But one countrywoman of yours — she would try anything. A good sport, that one. She had the lust for living, you know."

I hoped my eyes didn't give away the excitement I felt. So they knew her. But of course they would. Nobody who saw her once could ever forget her. She'd been here, hadn't she? Of course they'd know her. "That sounds like a friend of mine. She lives in Amsterdam."

But Amsterdammers do not meddle. The two men buried their noses in their drinks. The barkeep turned his back and busied himself with polishing some decorative copper pots.

I wondered if the police had already been to inquire about the man with pewter-colored hair and if they'd met with the same success. It wouldn't do, I saw, to be too curious without a good reason, one they could respond to with no feeling of betrayal.

So I tried a different tack. "I'm in the antiques business in New York." I fished out one of my cards. It said "North Shore Galleries." A perfectly good name for an antiques store. "I'm looking for a dealer named Frans Steen. I understand from my friend that he has good merchandise. I'm interested in buying, but I can't find him listed anywhere."

That was entirely different. Business is sacred in Amsterdam. In fact, Amsterdammers have told me themselves that they are the best merchants in the world. And they weren't bragging — merely stating the facts as they saw them.

The barkeep spun around and fixed me with an appraising eye. "Antiques? You are interested in them?"

"Oh, yes," I answered with genuine sincerity. After all, Seraphine had said Steen was an antiques dealer so I was *very* interested.

He put down the rag he was polishing with and leaned toward me, both hands on the bar. "My aunt has a shop in the Nieuwe Spiegelstraat. Her specialty is Delft tiles. They interest you?"

They certainly would if it meant gaining information. "Oh, yes."

"They're getting very hard to find," he cautioned. "I could ask her to set some aside for you."

"Please. The best two she has I'll trust her judgment. And could she ship them? And bill them to Mr. Gregor Olitsky?" I scribbled Gregor's name on my card and passed it to him. It would serve him right: although with Gregor's luck, they would turn out to be priceless. "But Steen is an expert in my specialty" — I thought wildly — "artifacts of the Dutch who settled Manhattan Island; and I'm told he has something he wants to sell me. Perhaps your aunt could help?"

He was already dialing a number on the telephone behind the bar. "She'll be happy to help. And perhaps when your business is done you could pay her a visit."

He handed me a card printed in Delft blue.

"Hello, Aunt Dorritt? I have an American lady here." There followed a barrage of Dutch which sounded like a machine gun in action. I didn't understand a word of it except that there were numbers and a pause while they were verified. When that was concluded, he continued. "This lady is looking for Frans Steen — she has business with him. Do you know where he's to be found?"

There were indignant noises at the other end. Frans Steen's name seemed to arouse strong emotions. The barman raised pained eyebrows and held the phone away from him, hand over the speaker. "My aunt knows him. So does everyone else in the trade. By reputation, anyway. She says if you go to the Amsterdam Printing Shop on Prinsengracht you'll find a girl who's carrying his child. You won't find him, though. He has a dealer's taste for the good things in life and they don't include hard work."

Noises were still coming out of the phone. He listened again.

"Try Keizersgracht 338, she says. Ask for

Mia van der Straeten. She'll know where to find him."

"Thank you so much."

"You can walk there in five minutes," they all assured me.

I wasn't so sure I could walk at all after I'd gulped down the rest of my jenever, choked on the flames that seared my throat, recovered as much of my composure as I could, and staggered out.

A light rain had begun to fall. Crowds of Amsterdammers thronged the sidewalks; and the streets were filled with battalions of cyclists, many carrying girls with demurely crossed ankles perched sidesaddle behind them. They charged forward, heedless of traffic lights, pedestrians, or even the trolley cars that clanged along in their midst.

As the bartender had promised, Keizersgracht was not far away. My walk took me past modest seventeenth-century buildings that had once housed tradesmen and artisans and on to the more patrician former merchants' homes lining the Keizersgracht; and I realized that Amsterdam is one of the few major cities in the world where the population still lives in the center of the town.

Number 338 turned out to be rather splendid. It rose five stories, directly facing the emperor's canal. There was a discreet brass plaque at the top of the steps leading to the front door. It was brand new and it said "Gallery 338 — Fine Art and Antiques."

I mounted the stoop and pressed the bell. The young woman who answered was very *dernier cri*: bright Fauve colors in clinging silk outlined her every feminine curve; but her hair was cropped short as a marine's.

Behind her in the hallway I could see large pastels of flower gardens and to the left a small parlor lined with more of the same except where the wall was interrupted by a fireplace braced by two handsome Chinese dogs. A fine lacquer desk covered with papers stood against the opposite wall.

"Mia van der Straeten?"

"No. But if you are interested in buying something . . . ?" Her eyes sparkled with a salesman's anticipation.

I presented her with one of my cards. "I should like to see Madame van der Straeten, if you please."

Apparently my card passed muster because she disappeared up the stairs and presently I could hear a soft feminine murmuring from above. Then there was the sound of brisk footsteps and a large blond woman descended as gracefully as if she were floating. I could tell that she would tower over me, but there was nothing masculine about her. Her face was as large and soft as her body, and I liked her on sight.

"Mrs. Willum, how nice to meet you." She gave me her hand. "You did the portrait of Gainsborough Brown, didn't you? I've always admired it."

My biggest claim to fame. Wasn't it ironic? Because I'd loathed Gainsborough Brown.

"I confess to everything," I told her.

We both laughed.

"Come in, come in." She motioned me into a room behind the formal little parlor. "It's more comfortable here than talking in the hall. See? So sit down. There on the sofa. And we will chat. Will you be long in Amsterdam?" She was too polite to ask immediately what I wanted of her. It was typical of Amsterdam good manners.

"I saw your plaque outside," I temporized. "As a gallery person, I thought I would like to meet you."

"Ah, yes. So you knew Gainsborough Brown? Yes, that is so interesting, I think."

"The North Shore Galleries still represents his estate."

"So I understand. We have occasional exhibitions by American artists at 338. We are hoping for one next year. The artist's representative has just been here, finalizing arrangements. The Dutch are fond of American work, you know. I'd like so much to have an exhibition of Gainsborough Brown one day. Do you suppose it could be arranged?"

It was a question I heard all the time. Wretched as the late artist had been in person, his work was still in great demand.

"I would have to speak to Mr. Olitsky. Amsterdam might interest him."

Gregor was a stern judge of who was or was not allowed a Brown exhibition.

Her big, pale blue eyes widened with pleasure beneath blond eyelashes. "That would be so kind of you. But forgive me for talking business — you did not come for that. What can I do for you?"

I took a deep breath. "Actually, I'm here to throw myself on your professional mercies."

"My what?" She was astonished.

"Well, it's a gallery matter. Did you ever meet a friend of mine named Seraphine Braceley?"

The large, kindly face paled a little and she didn't answer.

So I went ahead. "She sent us a painting from Amsterdam, which we did not solicit. Now the courier by whom she sent it has disappeared — and so has she."

I thought she whispered "I'm sorry," but I wasn't sure.

"The police are investigating — police on two continents, I imagine. And we're in the middle. We have no proof that she sent us the painting. It didn't even belong to her — we think it was still the property of the artist, Sandro Corsini. A mess. You see our position?"

She made sympathetic noises, watching me from beneath lowered lashes. "Most unfortunate." Then she looked up, directly into my eyes. Something about her expression made me think of a man before a firing squad. "But what can I do to help?"

I kept it to two words. "Frans Steen."

She must have been bracing herself ever since she saw my card, because she didn't show the least surprise. "Frans Steen. I see." She didn't say anything for a full minute, thinking it over. And in the end her scruples were outweighed by her business sense: Gainsborough Brown won the day.

"Come. We will talk upstairs." And she stood up carefully and led me up the blue-carpeted stairs, her fashionable long brown skirt swinging against beautiful brown leather boots that seemed too young for her.

She walked ahead into a long green salon in what was obviously her living quarters. It was a large room looking out on the canal.

The carpeting was peacock blue to echo the color of the velvet upholstery. Dark seventeenth-century Dutch landscapes covered the walls with a sea of windmills, skaters, and black-and-white cows. At the far end of the room stood a large trestle table behind which I could see ancient blue-and-white Delft tiles set in the wall of a modern kitchen.

The table was set for two. I recognized the wineglasses as French — their special blue could only have been hand blown at Biot.

Mia excused herself and stepped into the hall, where I heard her whispering to someone upstairs. There was a muffled rattle of footsteps and a young man burst into the room.

He was no more than thirty or so, casually dressed in jeans and a red sweater. He stopped short just inside the doorway, his bold eyes giving me a frank going over. He did not look apprehensive or nervous.

She put her big hand on his arm. "Frans, my love, this is Persis Willum and she's come about your friend Seraphine."

"That bitch."

"You don't have to say that. I know it was all over between you; and that is all that matters." She turned to me. "Frans and I have been partners off and on for many years — we were even in business once in New York City.

Antiques. Very successful and we've worked together since, off and on. Now I became an art dealer and Frans will do the antiques. You saw our sign?" She obviously felt that this short history explained the odd coupling and that the sign was an official blessing.

But I sensed something more. "You're protecting him from the police, aren't you? That girl downstairs doesn't know he's here."

She looked at me pleadingly. "He has done nothing. Just a matter of some checks long ago. But that trouble could be brought up again, with the police looking for your friend. It was a matter of a small business transaction — nothing very important. But the Dutch police are sometimes tough. And it would not be good for our image if he were arrested. A petty matter, that's all it was."

And problems with small checks ever since, I wondered?

Her business instincts were still at work. "So you will not say he is here if he speaks to you about your friend?" And — she didn't have to add — if I remembered to speak to Gregor about Gainsborough Brown.

"There's no reason why I should mention it."

"Good." She turned to Steen. "So you will help Mrs. Willum, Frans."

"Why should I? To please you? Are you

ordering me?" He was a short-tempered fellow and he glared at her malevolently. "There are other women who would be glad to have me, you know."

She was frightened by that. Then she recovered. "No one will take care of you as I do. You know that. So don't be a fool."

His feral eyes slipped away from hers. "She was just a drunken tramp I picked up in a pub...."

She interrupted. "That's not what you told me. You said it was she who picked *you* up ... that she'd heard you were a 'finder.' " She turned to me to explain. "A 'finder' travels around to places nobody else would go and buys things to sell to other dealers. A sort of legman. Country furniture is Frans's specialty. He knows every back road in the Netherlands, Belgium, and France by heart."

"Anyway, she wouldn't let me alone. And not just because I was a 'finder,' believe me. Couldn't get enough, if you know what I mean." I had the distinct idea that I did know. What, I wondered, could two women like Seraphine and Mia see in him?

"I mean, a woman like that coming on to me and pretending it was for antiques ... who was she kidding? Lost villages, she kept talking about. As if I believed ..." Then he saw Mia's expression and stopped. "Well, maybe it was true. That's all she talked about, anyway."

Antiques? Lost villages? Not Seraphine's style at all. And since when did a woman with Seraphine's looks have to make up stories to get a man?

I looked at him and tried to disguise my loathing. Had Seraphine really sunk to the level of third-rate Romeos like this one? It didn't seem possible.

"You didn't say you'd met her in a pub." Mia was chiding him like a mother. "You told me it was in the Waterlooplein, the Flea Market. You said she was going around to all the dealers asking about 'finders.'"

"Well, maybe. I forget. Anyway, she didn't have any money, Mia. I told you that." He seemed to feel that this would reassure her.

I looked at his light brown hair, artfully arranged to fall over his crafty blue eyes. I looked at his skintight jeans and his insinuating smile. And I marveled. This man was trash. The sound of the rooster crowing throughout the land was the sound of the likes of Frans Steen.

"She was staying in a fisherman's house outside of town ... to escape her social life, she said — but I never believed it. She never took me there, anyway. I tell you, she had no money.

She wore this enormous ring, but it was obviously a fake. And when we were together here in Amsterdam, she took me to this crummy hotel."

"Where?"

"A hotel called the Friendly. A fleabag. Near the museum."

Seraphine in a crummy hotel? Wanting to escape her social life? Living in a fisherman's shack?

"Were you with her at the Tapperij Iijsbercht last week?"

"No."

"Did she mention a Dr. Joosten? Did you ever see her with a man with gray hair?"

Two emphatic "no's." But then, he would be eager to reassure his mistress.

And she now decided that it was time to change the subject. "I think we must offer you lunch," she said sweetly. "A beer perhaps? With some herring? Maybe *broodjes* with a *borreltje* would be different. Yes, I think so. You cannot refuse."

She was convinced that her lover had nothing more to hide and relieved that it was over. But I knew better.

She floated out into the kitchen and began the ritual rattling of china and silverware. "So my friend was poor?" I asked softly, when I was sure Mia couldn't hear.

"I would have married her otherwise, you know," Steen answered. "Although she said she was getting money. But you can't believe them when they say that. Still, she had that book."

"What book?"

"She said it was her fortune. And her life insurance. I don't know what she meant. I got a look at it once, although she hid it like it was worth a million dollars."

"What was it? An address book?" Lovers, I supposed.

"Symbols, I think. I couldn't make sense of it. But she scratched my face like a wildcat when she found out I'd seen it."

Symbols? "Do you remember any of them?"

"No names. Just letters and initials. I remember the first line . . . AFM-MC and four numbers, I don't remember what they were. She was onto me before I could really make anything of it. She was like a maniac, so I guess it was important, whatever it was. But I never got my hands on it again. She was an odd one, that one."

"Why odd?" It was the last word I'd have chosen for Seraphine, somehow. Different, maybe. But odd?

"Well, she kept a gun in her purse, for one thing. Also drove me crazy wanting to go on trips with me — it's no good to have a woman in tow — you're dealing mostly with other women . . . farming women. . . ."

"Yes, I suppose it's hard to strike a bargain with one woman while you have another one along. Did you ever take her?" I wasn't paying much attention. I was thinking about the book. And the gun.

"Once. To the Ardennes. Did some business, but when we got to Rubigny she made such a fuss that I brought her back and never took her again."

"So how did it end?"

"End? Are you crazy? No woman ends with me." We were both keeping an eye out for Mia like the conspirators in *Julius Caesar*. "I went on a finding trip. When I got back, she was gone. I looked for her in all the usual places, but she had disappeared. Nobody would say anything."

Mia was calling from the other end of the room. "Come. Your 'snack' as the Americans say, is ready." Frans dashed over to help. The perfect courtier.

She kissed him fondly. "He is so good to me," she said. "He will be a good partner."

I hoped so. But I was really thinking that she'd better keep her money in a safe.

It was during lunch that Mia made her proposal.

I was munching on my *broodjes,* wonderful cheese-stuffed rolls, and they were stabbing away at their silvery herring and downing Dutch beers when her cheeks suddenly flushed and her smile turned challenging.

"I think I will drive Mrs. Willum out to see your love nest. Where did you say it was — that fisherman's shack?"

Steen began to choke on his herring. It was several heartbeats before he could answer. "I didn't. It was Marken. But I told you I was never there."

"No matter. I want to see her house for myself. This romantic place." She turned to me. "You would like to come?"

I definitely would. I couldn't imagine Seraphine in anything less than a four-star hotel or spa — certainly never in a fisherman's shack.

"Good. I will have you back by five. It's not far. I know this village. It is a place where artists like to go and paint — very colorful."

Steen continued to protest. He was doubtless afraid she would throw him out on the street after viewing the actual scene where his lover had lived. Women are like that.

But she would not relent. "I know you — you have a passkey. Do you think I believed all that about finding her book? You went to her house and snooped — that's how you found it. Took money, too, I don't doubt. I know about those keys: if you can't buy something at your price, you open the barn door and steal it."

In the end, he handed it over.

So we descended the blue-carpeted stairs, Steen still keening as loudly as he dared behind us, and climbed into Mia's car, which was wedged into an impossibly small space along the canal. She stepped fiercely on the starter and with two turns of her muscular arms we were out and off. She hadn't even glanced in her rear-view mirror.

"It is better if he's not too sure of himself this time. We've been through this before," she said as we wheeled into the middle of the traffic.

I looked at her set expression and thought — this time he'd better watch out.

The rain had stopped and there were patches of cold blue between the large, white, fast-moving clouds that raced across the sky. The streets we took were new to me. Dozens of trolleys picked their way carefully through the automobile and pedestrian traffic: gaily painted houseboats had their curtains open to show comfortable rooms inside. Mia wove in and out of traffic in a series of death-defying moves. Like most European women, she drove like a Grand Prix driver.

Once out of the city, she paused long enough to allow me to climb the wall of the dike and stand briefly on the path at the top, the wind tearing at my hair as I stared out at the rolling sea.

Then it was on again through the nearly empty countryside to Marken, where we parked on the outskirts of the village next to a tour bus full of shivering foreigners.

We left the car there and wound our way on foot into the canal-laced village. The wind was relentless, ferocious. I saw that there were no boats in the small harbor and I pitied the poor fishermen who were out on a day like this.

Three or four rows of tiny, bright-painted houses snuggled together in the village like sparrows on a telephone wire. At another time they might have seemed bewitchingly attractive in their bright blue-green paint: today they were only pathetic.

We headed toward a small café that tried to protect the port from the sea. "Come, we will have a coffee and see what we can find out. None of these houses have numbers, and Frans pretended not to know."

It was no more than a block or two; but by the time we arrived I was a sort of animated icicle.

The little café was the scene of frantic activity. All the tourists, after a first taste of the wind, had headed for the same shelter and were ordering everything they could think of in the way of alcohol. The place grew noisier with every drink.

As soon as our coffee arrived, Mia tackled the red-cheeked waitress. "Do you know the American woman who lives here? Do you know her house?"

"I'm new. But I will ask."

She crossed the room and spoke to the equally ruddy-cheeked young man behind the cash register, that bastion of power in every European café. He studied us suspiciously before approaching. "You are asking about an American? I'm sorry, but we are all new here . . . the entire staff. We change at the end of the summer season. I'm so sorry."

But Mia was not impressed. "It will be the empty house, I think. You see, I am leasing it but I want to see it first, naturally. It would be too bad if I couldn't see it today. You see, the agent has given me the key." And she flashed the passkey at him.

As usual, business won the day. "You want to rent it? Oh. Well, it's that one there — the bright blue."

"Thank you."

"My God," Mia said as we finished our coffee and prepared to leave. "Have you ever seen such respect for privacy? Such discretion? That's the Dutch for you."

We braved the wind once more. This time it was behind us and it swept us along like leaves tumbling along a Manhattan sidewalk in November. I was shaking in my lightweight raincoat — I'm never properly dressed for the European weather. Mia was comfortably wrapped in a down jacket.

I thought Frans Steen's key would never open the door but after a struggle it finally did and we stepped gratefully inside.

The whole, narrow, single-story house was about one-eighth the size of the foyer of the house Seraphine had shared in Gull Harbor with Etienne Dehorter.

"Living room," Mia said, impersonal as a real-state agent conducting a tour. But I noticed that her eyes were everywhere.

The living room was sparsely furnished with what must have been the original fisherman's sofa, side chairs, and tables. Seraphine had made no effort to replace them or to make the place more livable. A few English newspapers were scattered about, a down jacket was flung over a chair, nothing else of interest.

"Bedroom," Mia said, continuing the tour. There were plenty of clothes tossed carelessly over the bed, which wasn't made up. I was glad to see that she had at least brought her own sheets: they were Porthault. The clothes had the designer look I always associated with Seraphine: but they were not new. Two much-traveled suitcases stood against the wall, like porters awaiting orders.

"Bathroom." It was about the size of a spice closet and overflowing with the sort of mess I remembered from her school days — perfumes, makeup, shampoos, unidentified medicines. And towels draped along the edge of the tub.

"Kitchen." A few appliances, a minuscule ancient refrigerator and a hot plate for cooking. A half-empty cup of coffee nurtured its dregs on the counter. Dirty dishes in the sink. Seraphine had never been brought up to keep house for herself.

"Now that I've seen the place, I feel better," Mia pronounced. "He'll be a lot more comfortable with me. This is scarcely Frans Steen's style."

Nor was it Seraphine Braceley's.

And clearly she could not have intended it to be — at least, not permanently. To have stayed one minute in such a place meant that she was either dead broke or in temporary hiding . . . or both.

Chapter 10

It was just five-thirty when we returned to Amsterdam. Mia dropped me off in front of the Friendly Hotel, which didn't interest her at all. She had no further curiosity about the scenes of Steen's crimes with Seraphine . . . all she needed was one look at the Friendly's exterior to feel reassured.

"Horrible," she announced, as I climbed out of the car. "Places like this give Amsterdam a bad name. Nobody in his right mind would stay here. I can't imagine why Frans would set foot in a place like that."

She'd never set eyes on Seraphine Braceley. If she had, she'd know the answer.

But she was right about one thing — the Friendly was the last place on earth where anyone would look for a person like Seraphine or anyone else I knew. It must have been the cheapest hotel in the city, basically a converted seventeenth-century house that rose narrowly two rooms wide across the front but deeper in back. A TV screen mounted outside above the front door monitored arrivals and (more importantly I suspected, judging by the quality of the place) surreptitious departures.

"Thank you for lunch, Mia. And the trip to Marken. You have my card: if anything turns up that would be helpful . . ."

". . . you mean if she comes back. But she won't, you know . . . Frans is with me to stay. But if anything turns up about Gainsborough Brown — if you can speak to Olitsky . . ."

"I promise to let you know."

We said good-bye and she took off in a flurry of scorched rubber, eager to return to her beloved, while I climbed the indoor-outdoor carpeting that covered the steep steps to the Friendly's door.

The reception desk turned out to be in what I would have thought was the basement if a scattering of armchairs and tables and a small garden visible through the back windows hadn't suggested that this was the lobby. A television on the bar was sending off shafts of green light, a coffee machine burbled on a hot plate and a French song about falling snow and unrequited love drifted up from a radio beneath the counter. The whole place smelled like McDonald's. A single sad-eyed Tunisian presided over it all.

"Breakfast is served here, and hamburgers

any time of the day or night. You will like the prices," he assured me dispiritedly in French. "But the weather . . . I have not seen sunshine for two years. That is why the Dutch all wear eyeglasses: their vision is ruined. There is always darkness."

I hadn't noticed. But now that he mentioned it, it was indeed dark outside, and all day long there had been intermittent showers.

He emerged from behind the desk. "I will carry your bag — you will never manage the stairs otherwise. If you like the room you can come back down and register." There was a strong implication that I would not like the room and that I would not register.

"I don't have luggage," I told him. "A friend said I could have her room for the night."

As I expected in a place like this, he evinced neither surprise nor curiosity. Nothing, I knew, would shake his resigned acceptance of the futility of life in a country where it was never light. "Your friend's name?"

I told him. But he didn't recognize it. "Here they don't always give a real name. What does she look like?"

That was a different matter. "Ah, the American lady. Your friend? So nice. So beautiful. A face like Catherine Deneuve." The thought of Catherine Deneuve brought a few bars of another love song, delivered in an off-key and lonesome bass.

Two seconds later we were climbing the torturously narrow spiraling stairs to the third floor and he was struggling with a plastic card designed to open the door.

"You would let just anyone into her room like this?" I couldn't believe it.

"Only you. Because you speak French like Marlene Dietrich — so you are A.O.K. I am a good judge. It is my profession." His tone was as lugubrious as if there had been a recent death.

The part about Marlene Dietrich was a stunning blow. I would have thought, if anything, that my accent was American: and it was my fondest hope — unrealistic though I knew it to be — that I would one day speak with no accent at all. But German? Surely not. "I'm an American."

His brown eyes were infinitely sad. "Ah, well, that can't be helped. I will call you Marlene."

What could I say? It was that kind of place.

He had the door open now and waved me inside. The room was clean enough, but every bit as dreary as I had expected. Everything in it — curtains, walls, rug, bedspread — was dingy brown. Two front windows offered a view of the row of neglected houses across the street, each with bicycles chained to their front stoops. There were piles of plastic garbage bags piled along the sidewalk and papers stuffed randomly into trash baskets that leaned drunkenly at intervals. What curtains I could see in the windows opposite looked frayed and tattered.

"*Bienvenue,*" the Tunisian said dejectedly. "The room is paid for through this week. There is a small balcony, in front. But it is only big enough to hang the Dutch flag."

There wasn't much of Seraphine in this place. Just a comb and brush and toothpaste in the bathroom and a large towel. She could never have stayed longer than overnight.

Just long enough for her assignations. And phone calls? I didn't remember a telephone in Marken.

I could see an envelope in the scrap basket. It was from *Life,* and it was addressed to Seraphine. I could also see that it was empty.

"There is a view of the houses across the street that is not too bad." He stepped to the window and gazed out hopefully.

Across the room I saw a crumpled piece of paper under the table that held a telephone and quickly scooped it up and into my handbag.

"I won't be staying, thank you," I said.

"I didn't think so," replied the melancholy Tunisian.

We both crept cautiously back down the

stairs and he summoned a taxicab for me.

As we drove off, I took the paper from my bag and smoothed it out.

It was covered with Seraphine's big writing. There were two names, both crossed out. One was Sam Swann. The other was Howard Roth.

And there were two sets of letters and numbers. One was FB-AR and four numbers. The second was C-SS and four different numbers.

I recrumpled the piece of paper and put it back in my bag.

In a very short time we were at the Eureka, which was a pretty fine hotel after all.

When I stepped into the Eureka it looked as luxurious as the Europe. Such is the power of contrast.

The manager was lying in wait for me with a message. "A Mr. Olitsky has been trying to reach you." He glanced at his message pad. "You are to call him no matter what the hour." Since I felt as if I had just returned to civilization, I gave him a big smile and went happily to my room to return Gregor's call.

There was none of the usual panache in his voice when he answered.

"Where have you been, Persis? I've been calling every hour on the hour."

"Looking for Seraphine. You sent me here to find her — don't you remember?"

There are times when Gregor doesn't think of anyone but himself. This was one of those times.

"Well," he said, "you don't have to look anymore. That's why I've been trying to reach you. They've found her. She was dumped out of a car on one of those roads near De Gaulle airport, shot with her own gun. They didn't find her right away because she was stuffed in a garbage bag and they thought she was trash, which she sort of was, you know. Withers has arranged for your ticket on the next KLM flight out. I need you here . . . at once. It's a hell of a mess."

All this time I'd been wandering around Amsterdam she was lying dead at the side of a road outside Paris.

"When did it happen?"

"The police aren't sure, but they think it was shortly after she got the painting on the plane. Not pleasant to think of her lying there all that time, is it? It wasn't until the garbage people came along . . ."

"Stop it — I don't want to know."

But Gregor was a pragmatist. "You'll have to know some time. So pack up and get out of there. You can imagine what it's like here, with the police and the media and the collectors. This is no time for you to be in Amsterdam."

The way he said it, you'd think it had been my idea.

"I can't believe it. Not Seraphine." But strangely enough, I wasn't surprised. I might even have been expecting it.

"Funny thing," Gregor was saying. "Her handbag was cleaned out, but she was still wearing the Winston Reed diamond."

Dehorter had given her the emerald-cut ten-carat blue diamond as an engagement ring. It was said at the time that he'd paid a lot for it because of its rare intense blue color. I'd forgotten, but I now remembered that she'd rarely been seen without that ring, which she loved. She pretended it was a fake to insure that it wouldn't be stolen. And she swore she'd starve to death before she'd sell it.

"And there's one more funny thing," he went on. "You won't believe this. She was covered with a bouquet of red roses."

Seraphine shot with her own handgun. Still wearing her diamond. And covered with . . .

"Roses?"

"Exactly. Seems somehow fitting, doesn't it?"

"I'm not sure," I told him. "Anyway, I'll be right there. You can count on it."

And I began to pack.

Chapter 11

I threw my clothes into my suitcase, operating in a sort of stupor.

And all the way home on the plane all I could think of was Seraphine.

Why had I been willing to go to Amsterdam in the first place? It certainly wasn't because I wanted to pry into Seraphine's private life; her private affairs were none of my business. I was fond of her for what she was — not for what she did. And it wasn't because I thought for a minute that I could solve the mystery of Dr. Pieter Joosten: that was a matter for the police.

Then why had I acceded to Gregor's command? Why hadn't I refused?

I certainly didn't think Seraphine would ever be guilty of anything serious . . . she couldn't have changed that much. On the other hand, there was the dark side of this city — the side that sheltered all manner of society's outcasts and attracted the dispossessed and disturbed. Was that what had drawn her to Amsterdam to meet her final fate in a frenzy of self-destruction that ended outside an airport in France? Had she fallen so far through the cracks in today's society? I knew for certain that the Seraphine of my youth had never considered the real consequences of what she did — not even of her marriage to Dehorter. But still . . .

She'd done something unacceptable by Gull Harbor standards of proper conduct in sending the notorious nude to the exhibition. She'd embarrassed her family and friends. She'd generated unattractive publicity, which she knew perfectly well was a sin by our standards.

She'd flouted the sacred rules.

So why had I been willing to go?

There could only be one answer. I'd gone to Amsterdam to find an alibi for Seraphine, alive.

Was I now going back to Gull Harbor to find an alibi for her, dead?

I wondered all the way home.

Chapter 12

Gregor was pale and unstrung when I finally tracked him down.

Tracking him hadn't been easy. His faithful drunken secretary, Withers, of the contradictorily infallible memory, had been instructed to guard his whereabouts with her life and she was prepared to do so. And to prove it, she gave me a hard time until I lost my temper.

"He *called me* last night. He *ordered* me to come back. You arranged the tickets, remember?"

So she gave in and instructed me in whispers that he was at the Gull Harbor Polo Club having a delayed breakfast.

What he was actually doing, of course, was hiding out.

He was sitting at one of the tables in the glassed-in section overlooking the polo field, his nose in the club handbook, which was called, not surprisingly, *Rules of the Game*. I knew it was a ploy to keep anyone from bothering him: Gregor rarely reads anything more taxing than a best-seller or the society columns.

I had to admit that the club was a clever place to hide. It was the last place anyone would expect to find him, as he was devoutly opposed to strenuous exercise.

"Why are you hiding here, Gregor?"

He ignored it. "Great game, this. Did you know that the first formally recorded match was in Middlesex in 1869 between the ninth regiment of Lancers and the tenth regiment of Hussars? Of course the Tibetans and Mongols and Chinese have been swinging mallets for centuries and everyone knows that Darius's soldiers played in Persia twenty five hundred years ago."

"I didn't know," I said, taking a chair and easing my tourist-class-stiff body into it. Gregor never sent me any way but tourist. Naturally, he himself traveled first class. "What are you doing here, anyway?"

"I'm thinking about taking up the game. It came to me just this morning. Admittedly, it will be a big initial outlay for all that equipment — helmets, crop, spurs, saddle and bridle, breeches, shirt, mallet." He was already imagining himself in all the gear.

"What about the ponies?" I asked, cruelly. "You'll need a minimum of six to play; and you have to have the best if you want to play here. The Argentine ponies are expensive, you know. They eat a lot, too. And you'll need grooms, and stall space, and a van. And aren't you a little old to start?"

He was insulted. "What about Dehorter? He's older than I am." He waved toward a mounted figure that had just cantered out onto the field, swinging a bamboo mallet and taking practice shots at a plastic ball. "He's at least my age."

"Older," I said. "He's in his seventies now."

"Well, there's your answer."

Dehorter wheeled his pony around as we watched, reins in his left hand, mallet in his right. The pony's head was jerked high, and only the martingale kept him from going over backward. Man and beast then set off down the field in furious pursuit of the ball.

"He rides like a sausage," I remarked sourly. "I'll bet he ruins a dozen good ponies a year."

Another figure had taken the field, this one small and slight. "Christine Kelley," Gregor told me gleefully. "So she's taken up polo now, has she? Determined to catch him, that's obvious."

It didn't interest me. "How can you think about these people and taking up polo when Seraphine is dead?"

He sighed. "The way things are going in my life, it's as good a time to take up polo as any."

I stared out the window at Seraphine's ex-husband returning down the field at about a hundred miles an hour while Kelley gathered up her mount to join him. I was remembering the first time I'd seen him. How handsome he'd been, tearing through every chukker with the passion of a man obsessed. What he lacked in horsemanship, he'd made up for in energy. Had his team won? Who had they been playing against? I couldn't remember. All I recalled was the sleek good looks that had bedazzled Seraphine when they were introduced after the game. And I wondered if Seraphine, surrounded by her usual crowd of admirers, had seemed to him at the time to be another game to be won

"He's still good-looking." I admitted it grudgingly, watching his ferocious attack on the ball and the ruthless way he rode Kelley off as they careened down the field.

Gregor wasn't listening. "I don't see why I need six ponies — a period is only seven and a half minutes long, according to this, and there are only six periods."

"Because horses can't go at that speed for longer than seven and a half minutes, even though they're specially bred for the game."

"Oh, well." He gave it all up. "It was just a thought."

"Yes. You'd better stick to winter balls and

summer tennis. Now tell me about Seraphine."

He turned his back on the window, definitely through with polo. "They think she drove to Roissy with Joosten and spent the night in his room at the PLM motel near the airport. Next morning she vamped an Air France employee to get the painting aboard the plane — could have done it while Joosten was fussing with the tickets . . . she must not have wanted to leave it to Joosten — and that's the last anyone knows until her body was found. They say Joosten was scheduled to fly out of Amsterdam the night she called, but he canceled in favor of the Roissy flight the next day. Witnesses remember seeing her around the ticket area — she was hard to forget. Nobody remembers seeing Joosten."

So far it made sense. She'd met Joosten by chance at the restaurant, found him attractive, persuaded him to change his flight, and driven to Paris to spend the night with him. Then she'd seen to it personally that the painting got aboard the plane. He'd still arrive in New York in plenty of time for the conference and he could still be her errand boy.

"And then somebody killed her. Do they know why?"

He shook his head and examined his gold cuff

links. I knew why he wouldn't look at me: he was afraid I might cry. While he himself didn't have any qualms about public displays, he loathed such things in others. Certainly floods of tears at the polo club were high on his list of things simply not done.

"Who knows, Persis?" He tried for a joke. "Maybe she wasn't fun in bed anymore." He saw my face and apologized. "Sorry. Didn't mean it. The only theory *they* have — meaning the police — is that she may have seen Joosten kidnapped. *If* he was kidnapped. It couldn't have been robbery — there was the ring."

Industrial espionage and kidnapping — could Seraphine have inadvertently gotten herself mixed up in something like that?

"And Joosten, Gregor — any word about him?"

"Not that they've told me. Seems to have registered and then vanished into thin air. Hard to manage these days, you'd think. Or someone managed it for him."

I remembered the car in the bay. "If he was kidnapped in front of Seraphine at De Gaulle, how could he have registered in Gull Harbor and who picked up his rented car and how did it end up in the bay?"

"Beats me," he said resignedly.

"And the diamond — was it the real one?"

"It was. So they've ruled out robbery."

"And the roses. Why?"

"God alone knows. Maybe Joosten gave them to her — it's the prevailing theory; But my guess is that the police are as baffled as we are."

"Who will get the *Olympia?* It's worth a lot of money."

"Sandy hasn't laid claim to it, so I suspect it will go to her family, along with the ring and anything else that's left. Our appraisers put a price on the *Olympia* yesterday. Two million, they figure. At the least."

A motive for murder?

"Listen, Gregor, you can't hide out here all day. We have to go back to the gallery and face the music."

"Oh, can't I? look here, Persis, we're in possession of a two-millon-dollar painting with no clear provenance. Corsini could probably lay claim to it, but he hasn't — and that's odd. You were at Harrington House asking for a man who disappeared, and *that* looks odd. The situation is very serious."

"I know." I stared out the window at Dehorter, who was riding off the field, presumably to change his sweat-lathered pony for a fresh one.

I stood up. "Come on, Gregor. You really can't stay here. We have to do something about the *Olympia*. Isn't Henrietta Braceley suing you?"

"I took it off display the minute the news came that Seraphine was dead. The police didn't like it, but they couldn't stop me."

"Where is it now?"

"In my office until my lawyers give me instructions."

"I'd feel better if it were out of the gallery entirely. Well, let's get out of here. We haven't got all day. We have things to do."

"Like what? There's nothing but trouble out there."

"Like pay our respects to Henrietta Braceley. We're not barbarians, after all."

"I am." He rose to his feet. "I'm going to my club in town; no one will look for me there. You go pay your respects to the dragon lady. I'll send her buckets of flowers instead."

He meant it. I was going to have to face the bereaved mother alone. It was like sending a gladiator into the arena without his sword.

Chapter 13

I knew the Braceley house by heart from the old days. And it looked exactly the same — a classic Gull Harbor white clapboard country house.

It had been built in the twenties, designed by everybody's then favorite architect, Julian Peabody. He was the only one to engage in those days if you wanted to be gentry, because he *was* gentry and he knew about including all the things other architects neglected, like the right number of third floor servants' bedrooms, a servants' dining room, a safe for valuables when you were off in Aiken or up in Saratoga or traveling abroad.

The Braceleys had bought it in the fifties and had the good sense to leave it alone, redecorating, when necessary, in the same style. After all, buying such a house was part of upward mobility.

I remembered that there was a lot of bright English chintz in the drawing room, where the walls were glazed a pale peach — the first pale peach walls I ever remembered seeing. Today they are the rage. Every wall held horse paintings by George Stubbs and Raoul Millais and Munnings and other English equine artists, although no member of the Braceley family ever rode a horse to my knowledge until Dehorter appeared on the scene, when Seraphine made a few attempts to master the art of horsemanship, without notable success.

In those days the library walls had been painted a dark green and there were quantities of Audubon bird prints and more horses — also prints this time — and quantities of brown-and-blue Brunschwig & Fils fabric. The cabinets were full of blue-and-white China Trade plates and bowls, and there were flowering plants everywhere.

Knowing Henrietta and her mania for fitting into Gull Harbor, I didn't expect anything to have changed much. She'd bought the house because it was "right," and I was willing to wager she'd be smart enough to leave it the way she found it because the right look was the slightly worn look. The Braceleys had been newcomers when they arrived but she'd always known exactly how to fit into the landscape.

And now, I thought as I crossed the driveway to the front door, Henrietta and all the Braceleys had almost achieved her goal. With foreigners and Yuppies and Wall Street whizz kids moving into the area, the Braceleys were on the brink of becoming Old Family. The first five unfortunate daughters had been banished and were not recently heard from, son Jordan had made his brilliant marriage, and that left only . . . Seraphine. Always Seraphine standing between them and total acceptance.

And now Seraphine had had the poor taste to get herself murdered.

I was shown into the library by the butler — it had been an Irish maid in the old days.

To my surprise I found both Henrietta and her son Jordan waiting. He was stationed before the fireplace, hands clasped behind his back like royalty. His mother was seated regally in a George III armchair.

Neither of them looked bereaved. Just cross.

"I'm so sorry about Seraphine," was all I could offer to their stony faces.

"It was nice of you to come," Jordan told me stiffly. His good-looking Braceley features were set and angry today.

Henrietta didn't waste time with niceties. "We're having her buried in France. There will be no service. Jordan's secretary has left to make the arrangements. There will be no flowers. No further uproar. Seraphine has caused quite enough uproar for one lifetime."

Jordan nodded agreement. "Missy and I have taken the children out of school. We had to, of course. They can't be exposed to all this. She's taken them to the house in Vail, even though it's not the season. We thought it best. "

I felt a fleeting pity for him. His wife and her family would hate all this.

Henrietta's face was cast iron. "This is very hard on Jordan. Seraphine had every opportunity and she threw it all away." She reached up and touched Jordan's arm tenderly. It was the only tender gesture I had ever seen her make. "Thank God for Jordan. He's given us four fine grandchildren. I hope they survive Seraphine's dragging our name through the mud."

Five older sisters had done it first, I thought. But I suppose Henrietta would merely have pointed out that at least they hadn't got themselves murdered.

I was very sorry I had come.

Jordan suddenly remembered his manners. "Port?"

"Please." I needed it. I'd never received a more frigid welcome anywhere.

Henrietta felt she should explain. "We're not seeing anyone, you know. You're an exception, because you were her friend."

Jordan filled three glasses from a cut-glass port pitcher. He studied mine thoughtfully before passing it to me, as if its ruby depths contained the answer to some question. "Father is in his room. He had an attack of angina when the news came," he said.

"Seraphine's fault," Henrietta snapped.

"I'm sorry. But do you think . . ."

He held up an imperious index finger to stop me. "This house must be kept tranquil. No anxiety. We are 'going to ground,' as they say. Father must not be disturbed. My children must be protected from the media circus Seraphine has stirred up."

"Has a doctor seen . . ."

Up went the finger again. All Jordan needed was a laurel wreath to play the role of emperor. "As my mother said, we made an exception for you. You've just returned from Amsterdam, haven't you? What did you find out?"

So that was why they'd made an exception of me.

His mother's hard little eyes gleamed with sudden vivacity. "What was she doing there?"

"I don't know," I answered, because it was true. "I can't answer that."

He looked to his mother for his cue. Then:

"You must have learned something," he said flatly. I remembered that among other things he was a lawyer. "You didn't go all that way for nothing."

The things I'd learned were the last things I was never going to tell them. They were furious enough at Seraphine without hearing about Frans Steen and the Friendly Hotel and the blue house in Marken. Besides, I didn't know what those things meant.

"I was organizing a Gainsborough Brown exhibition with Gallery 338 in Amsterdam."

Jordan Braceley set down his glass on the English cylinder desk and jammed his hands into the pockets of his brown tweed jacket. "I see." He and his mother exchanged glances again. Suddenly he looked like a typical Gull Harbor tycoon and I realized that he really was — in spite of his youth, he sat on the boards of the Waldheim and Harrison House and a half dozen companies I'd forgotten.

When he spoke his tone was dryly impersonal. "One reason we ask is that we'd like to know her recent state of mind. We received Seraphine's latest will by express mail shortly before this last unfortunate business. With it came this note. As you knew her so well, we wondered what you thought..."

He handed me the note. I recognized her bold scribble.

"It sounds like a suicide note. But of course that's not how she died. So we wondered what you thought — if you could shed some light..." Henrietta put in.

My hand began to tremble and the paper

jumped up and down so violently that I could scarcely read, large as the writing was. Finally I made it out.

"My Darlings," she had written with her typical gigantic flourishes, "I send you this thoroughly legal document at this time knowing that you would surely miss having it more than you will ever miss me."

I handed the note back to Jordan. I wondered if the pain in my chest was the pain of my heart breaking. Poor Seraphine. "You've showed this to the police?"

"Certainly not. After all, she didn't commit suicide, so it isn't pertinent."

Some tiny vestigial remnant of motherhood must still have existed in Henrietta because she needed to be reassured. "You don't think she would have killed herself, do you?"

"Of course not — don't be absurd, Mother," her son snapped. "You mustn't upset yourself."

But Henrietta had to know. "Could she have been afraid of being" — it was hard for her to say the word, and I didn't blame her — "murdered?"

I thought of the Friendly Hotel and of the fisherman's shack she wouldn't have been caught dead in.

And I wasn't sure.

I thought of her "life insurance." "No," I

said firmly, getting up to leave. "I don't think she was afraid of being murdered."

"Well," Henrietta said with some satisfaction, "at least they didn't get the Winston Reed diamond. So maybe she killed herself after all."

I doubted it. Seraphine wasn't the kind to put a gun to her head and pull the trigger and blow her beautiful face to bits.

Never in a million years.

Chapter 14

There was just time for a fast swing past Sam Swann's.

Sam lives in a big house with views of Long Island Sound from every window on the west side. It is built in a square around an atrium, which is in a state of noncompletion and bare of anything except some pebbles and an optimistic spotlight shining down on nothing.

"It's going to be sensational when it's done," Sam declared each time I visited, and had been declaring for at least ten years.

Sam edits her magazine out of her vast living room, which, as a consequence, is cluttered almost to the ceiling with papers, copy machines, fax machines, telephones, computers, typewriters, and assorted other objects having to do with publishing. There are also a secretary, a cast of "Famous Correspondent" refugees from other publications, and a whole roster of animals, including a demented foxhound, an elderly raccoon, and a pet chicken that seems to think it is a bald eagle.

The whole cast was assembled and milling around making noise when I knocked on the door. Receiving no answer, I let myself in.

It wasn't surprising that nobody heard my knock: the chicken was in full cry and so was the foxhound. Sam was leading this mixed orchestra with an unrestrained outburst of temperament, throwing sheets of copy paper about while upbraiding the entire roomful of Famous Correspondents in colorful language. Her fiery red hair had escaped from the rubber band that usually held it more or less in place and was flopping around like a mop, and I could have sworn I saw jets of steam coming out of the top of her head. Her long, slim body was thrashing back and forth as if she were in the throes of a seizure. It was a very impressive performance.

"How could you have let Francy James scoop us like that? How does she always get there first with her column? It's outrageous. What kind of journalists are you, anyway? That story was right here in our own backyard and we could have had it in this month's issue if any of you had been on the ball and acted like a professional journalist instead of the idiots you are."

One of the idiots objected. "You were too busy to talk to anyone, you said. We gave you Braceley's message to call her in Amsterdam. I kept a carbon. It's still right there on my desk."

There was much rummaging around until a yellow telephone message slip was resurrected and defiantly read aloud. "Three-forty-five P.M. Seraphine Braceley from Friendly Hotel, Amsterdam, to alert Swann that controversial painting about to blow lid off hospital benefit. Please return call."

"I never saw it — *never saw it,*" Swann shrieked furiously, snatching the paper from the writer's hand and tearing it to bits. "There's no note on my desk — never was. You're lying! Do you think I'd ignore a thing like that? Why didn't you follow up?"

"Have you forgotten — you went out of town the next day, and by the time you got back, we were past deadline."

"Well, God damn it, don't let it happen again. You're all probably working for that James creature behind my back, helping her to scoop me in my own backyard. I won't stand for it — you hear me?" She was wearing a sort of loose African robe under which she appeared to be doing a dance on hot coals and she hadn't bothered with shoes. Now she stamped her foot so hard that she cried out in pain. "God damn it — now look what you've done . . . now I'm a cripple, on top of everything else you've done to me."

All the nonhuman participants chimed in with whines and clucks of sympathy.

That was when she finally saw me.

"Persis — what are you doing here? We're just having a staff meeting, brainstorming on how to improve the magazine's timeliness. What can I do for you?"

I couldn't very well say you've already done it, but she had.

"Just stopped in to see how things were going. I suppose you're doing a big story on Seraphine's murder?"

With a last ferocious frown, she waved her staff back to work, and they scattered gratefully. "Only in a very dignified way, you may be sure. We're not a rag like that thing Francy James works for. I've assigned my top correspondent to the story. We'll handle it with kid gloves. After all, she was one of *us*." She was smiling winningly now and I was amazed at how lovely she was when she wasn't angry. Unfortunately she was angry most of the time. Maybe it went with the professional territory. More likely it was her love life — or lack of it. Sam was a confirmed lady bachelor. She'd never married; never showed any signs of even wanting to marry. And over the years she'd grown more testy as her magazine grew more successful. As the circulation went up, her spirits seemed to go down.

"Is that the only reason you came by?" she asked now. "I hear you've been in Amsterdam.

Maybe you have something new to add to the story? Did you find out anything I should know?"

I shook my head. "Nothing. And I won't stay. I can see how busy you are." I was already backing up to make my exit.

"Well, don't forget me if you think of anything. You don't know how important it is."

I knew one thing: Seraphine had telephoned to warn Sam about the arrival of the *Olympia,* and she'd left the name of her hotel. There was only Sam's word that she never got the message.

I didn't know what that meant, but I knew it could mean something. And it probably wouldn't be good.

Chapter 15

There was a message from Ed Simms when I got home. Mrs. Howard, my "houseworker"— as she chooses to be known, and not without a certain accuracy — had pinned it to the Reynolds-wrapped dish of yesterday's chicken in wine she'd left for the cat's dinner. Mrs. Howard loves my cat, which she herself had bestowed on me and named "Isadore" Duncan, because "she's always jumpin' around."

She'd left cold meatloaf for me.

Her note said, "J. Edgar Hoover called — said you was to call back. Be sure to serve cat's dinner by 8 P.M. so it don't dry out."

"It's nice," I told Isadore, who was prancing on tiptoe around my legs, "to be loved."

"Oreaough," she replied, smiling graciously.

Mrs. Howard and I know from experience that the exquisitely refined Isadore eats only the most tender chicken (although, like Suzanne Valadon's cat, she prefers Beluga caviar) warmed to exactly the right degree. It must not be too hot, nor too dried out. And she would rather starve than touch a single morsel that wasn't fit for the most finicky human gourmet. She was now winding around me in dizzying circles like a tipsy chorus girl, pretending that she was starving to death; and I rushed to warm her dinner, even though I was perfectly aware that this fineness of appetite was an affectation, born as she was of pure alley cat parents. It was, in fact, in an alley that Mrs. Howard had originally found her.

Only after Isadore had eaten did I dare return Simms's call. My own cold meatloaf on its unappetizing bed of wilted lettuce could wait. Indefinitely.

Simms answered the phone himself. "FBI Art Squad."

"I can't believe you're still in the office. Don't you ever go home?"

"Press of business," he responded. "Trying to clean up my desk to get in a trip to Paris. Thanks for returning my call. I suppose you're chilling some champagne?"

"Hardly." I put down the phone for a second and slid the meatloaf onto Isadore's plate. "How about you?"

"Reorwww," Isadore said disdainfully, stalking on stick-straight legs into the other room.

"No smart remarks, please," I called after her.

Simms thought I was talking to him. "I wasn't planning to make any."

"Sorry — I meant the cat. So you're still in your institutional green office working. It must have to do with the painting at Gregor's gallery or you wouldn't be calling me."

"Perhaps." Simms never gave anything away for free, so I braced myself for what was surely coming. "You've been in Amsterdam, snooping around. What did you learn?"

But I knew him too well. "Is this to be a trade-off?" I demanded.

"Citizens are expected to volunteer helpful information to the law," he told me piously. "It is a citizen's duty."

I laughed. "As my revered grandmother used to say . . . horsefeathers. But we might do some horse *trading*. What do you say?"

I'd helped Simms out once or twice on art theft cases and we understood one another perfectly by now.

"You first," he said.

"Seraphine had a book that she guarded carefully. It had symbols and numbers in it. She called it variously her fortune and her life insurance, not that it helped her in the end if that's truly what it was. Did they find it, do you know?"

"Negative. First I've heard of it. Anything else?"

"She kept a room in a crummy hotel. For her assignations, I guess."

"We know. Probably nothing to do with anything."

"O.K. Your turn now. Ouch!" Isadore had returned and was climbing up my leg, claw by claw.

"You all right? O.K. Well, nothing earthshaking. But it's kind of interesting. And seeing as how you spent so much time trying to track down this Pieter Joosten, I thought you might want to know."

I pushed Isadore unceremoniously off my lap and she landed, yowling, with all four feet on the floor. "What about Joosten?" I could feel my heart begin to pound.

"I thought you might like to know about his passport." He said it indolently. We could have been discussing the weather.

Isadore leapt onto the back of a chair opposite me and stared at me with malevolent yellow eyes, awaiting an apology. "What about his passport?"

"It's a forgery," he said. "Good night. Enjoy your champagne."

And he hung up.

"Damn." There was no use calling him back; he wouldn't answer.

"Oeurrowww," said Isadore.

For once we were in complete accord.

Chapter 16

There were two other telephone calls that night. Isadore, who detests the telephone because it requires too much of my time, which she believes should be devoted to her, was furious.

The first was from Sandy Corsini. "How about coming by for a cup of tea tomorrow?" Sandy doesn't drink anymore. With his artistic temperament, it is probably just as well. Drinking might have absorbed the boundless peasant energies he now devotes to his work, work done in such painstaking technique that each painting takes months and sometimes years to complete.

"Love to." It was my first invitation since the divorce . . . Neither of Seraphine's ex-husbands had ever really forgiven me for being her friend. And I was more anxious to see him than he could possibly be to see me. There was the question of the *Olympia*.

"Four o'clock, then."

"I'll be there." Gregor would be thrilled to

let me off early if he thought I could find out why Sandy was so mum about the *Olympia* or if I could cement good public relations with the great artist or find something that would explain anything that was happening.

Next it was Etienne Dehorter — both ex-husbands in the space of five minutes. Was it coincidence, or was Seraphine's shade still hanging around directing the action?

"I saw you at the club this morning," Dehorter announced without preamble. "And I wonder — would you come by for a drink tomorrow evening after work?"

I didn't bother to ask why he wanted to see me for approximately the same reasons I hadn't asked Sandy. Anything I learned would be better than the nothing I knew now. "At six," I said. "If that's not too late."

"Perfect. I'll be expecting you."

It was my second first invitation within minutes, and I wasn't about to refuse either of them.

Jet lag had left me reeling with fatigue and I threw myself into bed as soon as I could. So naturally I was wide awake, eyes as open as if they were propped wide by toothpicks. Questions pounded around in my exhausted brain. Ed Simms's news, for example. What was the meaning of the false passport?

Not that there was anything strange about

false passports in Gull Harbor. It had begun with the hijacking of planes and the executions of Americans aboard. Many of those passports — manufactured by two imaginative and enterprising and quite legal ladies out West — listed the owners as being citizens of some made-up, nonexistent country to avoid their being punished by terrorists for being Americans. So it was clear that a false passport was easy to get.

The question was — why?

And all the other questions.

What was Seraphine doing in Amsterdam? Why had she been murdered? Why did she personally make sure that the painting was put aboard the plane? Who had murdered her? And who had sent her the bouquet?

The last time I looked at my clock it was six A.M. and I hadn't closed my eyes. But I must have fallen asleep after that, because I had a dream.

In my dream, the North Shore Galleries was being besieged by furious collectors demanding that the Collectors' Choice show be dismantled or face legal action. There was a furious mob of them, waving sticks and banners and threatening to mount Gregor's and my heads on pikes and march through the streets to show the populace what terrible people we were for putting the *Olym-*

pia on display and thus bringing dishonor on Gull Harbor.

It was a terrible dream. Luckily my alarm went off before they could have our heads; and Gregor and I were saved by the bell from the ignominy of being marched through the streets without our bodies.

Chapter 17

The delegation descended on the North Shore Galleries shortly before noon. Which just goes to prove that there is more to dreams than is generally acknowledged.

I couldn't believe my ears when I heard the commotion in the main gallery, and I dashed out to investigate.

Just as in my dream, they had Gregor backed up against the wall and were shouting threats at him. Lily Armbruster was acting as ringleader and chief spokeswoman. At least, she was making the most noise and addressing a pale and cornered Gregor in ringing tones that resembled somebody delivering a manifesto.

For Gregor to be faced with so many enraged clients en masse had to be an unnerving experience — and he was clearly just that — unnerved. Even, for once, speechless.

I rushed to help. "What's the trouble?"

They weren't exactly a mob carrying pikes, but the mood was the same. There wasn't a smile in the bunch.

"We want this entire exhibition closed down," Lily told me in tones of rising intensity. "This murder business is the last straw. We've had all we can take. We want our paintings back immediately and a public apology to the hospital and to us for the circus that has gone on around here in our names."

A quick survey of the room confirmed that they were all there, everyone who had lent a painting to the exhibition. Plus wives and supporters. It was an appalling situation.

"But the hospital is getting all the money," I protested. "Wasn't that the whole point of the exhibition?"

"That was the original idea," Lily admitted. She was looking particularly exotic today because in her haste to lead the mob she had forgotten to pin on all her curls, or else they had fallen off during her passionate oration, and she was therefore nearly bald. "But nobody dreamed it would end up like this, with that awful naked Seraphine Braceley getting herself murdered and police snooping into everyone's affairs and the press all over Gull Harbor, prying into everybody's business. Not that I couldn't have murdered her myself for sending that horrid painting and besmirching the quality of all our masterpieces. Anyway, this show must end or we'll sue you for every penny you have."

"That's right," cried the Greek chorus behind her, "it must end."

Townsend Smith, Howard Roth, and Simon Wheeler were practically foaming at the mouth. So were their wives. Randall McCoy was tomato red and all his veins were distended and pulsating. Pinky Williams and his wife were there for moral support, and looked personally insulted. Dehorter and Christine Kelley were also on hand, and even Sandy's assistant. I thought I caught a glimpse of Jordan Braceley, but I must have imagined it — the Braceleys had "gone to ground," hadn't they?

There were about forty people in all, including some I'd never seen before. I prayed that the unknowns weren't members of the press who'd managed to infiltrate the group.

Gregor's nerves had already been frazzled by events; now he looked as if he might faint.

I thought about my dream and looked around that big room at the magnificent paintings glowing on the white walls. How could such a scene as this be taking place before the splendor and dignity of Rembrandt, Cézanne, Matisse, Picasso, Renoir, Gauguin, Vermeer, El Greco, Monet, Whistler, Manet, and the rest of the masters gathered here?

The guards, alarmed by the number of people who had pushed their way in and by the raised voices and flushed faces, were alert, fingers on triggers. Suppose somebody made a wrong move? Suppose somebody got shot?

The desperateness of the situation gave me courage. I stepped forward and put my arm around Lily Armbruster's bony shoulders.

"Of course Gregor agrees with you — in fact we've already begun making arrangements. The show comes down. We felt it was only fitting in view of the latest developments." I didn't want to use the word "murder" and set them off again. "All that was holding us up was that we wanted to give you the courtesy of notifying you in advance. But since I see that you're all here, we can now take it down just as Gregor had planned."

"I had?" he whispered to me. Luckily they didn't hear because they were busy congratulating themselves.

"This has been very painful for everyone," I continued. "But the good news is that the Gull Harbor hospital will benefit by a quarter of a million dollars in gate receipts and contributions by individuals and corporations." Withers had produced the current figures just that morning and I thanked God for her industry.

They were mollified. "How wonderful," they told one another. "How perfectly marvelous. Such a good cause."

The mob atmosphere evaporated at once. The guards relaxed. There would be no major news "incident" today.

Lily Armbruster may have been disappointed to see her revolution evaporate, but like the born agitator she was, she swung with the changing tide. "On behalf of all the collectors represented in this exhibition I wish to express our gratitude to the North Shore Galleries for your tact in ending the show and for the great contribution you have made to the Gull Harbor hospital."

"Hear, hear," someone said in the background. There was a smattering of applause; and they all surged forward to shake Gregor's hand. On such slim threads do revolutions hang and are destinies decided.

"Close," Gregor said to himself. "Very close."

We almost made it.

They were beginning to leave. Quiet almost reigned again in the gallery. Gregor had taken a second to mop his brow with a great white handkerchief.

And then Withers appeared, whiter than ever under her usual layers of ghostly white powder. All of her Aztec-type beads were rattling. And she must have taken several extra swallows from the bottle she kept in her drawer because the whiskey fumes that preceded her could have caused a fire had anyone lit a match.

"Mr. Olitsky . . . oh, Mr. Olitsky . . . come quick."

Her appearance was so dramatic that conversation ceased instantly and we all turned to stare.

"What is it?" Gregor was frozen in mid brow-mop, stiff as a figure in a wax museum.

"Somebody's murdered the picture."

"What?"

"Seraphine Braceley — there's a big knife sticking right in her chest. Come see for yourself. And there are roses all over the place."

Gregor uttered a groan of despair. Everyone rushed forward. I signaled to the guards to bar the crowd from Gregor's office.

And through all the noise I clearly heard Lily Armbruster's voice.

"Serves the silly thing right," was what she said.

Withers's description was, as usual, accurate.

Seraphine-Olympia's arrogant gaze hadn't changed. She was still wearing one oriental slipper. She still had a thin black ribbon tied at her neck and a flower behind her left ear. She still wore a single wide bracelet. Her ankles were still crossed.

But now there was a Swiss army knife plunged hilt-deep into her bare left breast and a dozen long-stemmed red roses scattered on the floor below the painting.

It was a most macabre scene.

"How much somebody must have hated this painting," a small, horrified voice whispered. There was a strong odor of insanity in the room.

"How much somebody must have hated *her*." Gregor was whispering, too, awed by the savagery of it.

"Sick, sick, sick," was Withers's unstrung comment. "Maniacs, that's what we have here — maniacs. It's not normal."

"Call the police, Withers." I think Gregor said it to give her something to do, to keep her and everyone else from becoming unglued. He was a great believer in action of some kind, any kind, when things were going wrong.

So she did. And we sat and stared at the Seraphine-Olympia until they arrived, which didn't take long.

They stared, too, when they got there. A murdered painting was evidently no more an everyday occurrence for them than for us. It was the same two detectives who had been in the gallery so often by now that they were almost a part of the regular staff.

They studied the painting for a long time and examined the office meticulously. I don't know what they were looking for. If they found anything pertinent they didn't mention it.

"What do you think?" Gregor asked them when they were done.

"This sort of thing happens. Publicity of any kind brings out the loonies. You say you were in your office until the collectors arrived?"

Gregor and I took turns answering.

"Yes."

"And the painting was undisturbed?"

"Absolutely all right when I went outside to talk to everyone."

"Did anyone go into your office after you left?"

"I don't think so. But I suppose it's possible. There was quite an uproar. We might not have noticed. Our attention was on Mrs. Armbruster."

"You knew everyone in the crowd?"

"Not everyone. There were a few strangers who might have slipped in with the group. I was afraid they were Press."

They wrote everything down. "There won't be prints on the knife, of course. And it's the kind you can buy in any sporting goods or hardware store. Seems brand new. Is it unusual for paintings to be attacked like this?"

Gregor looked at me: I'm supposed to be the scholar. So I answered.

"No, I'm sorry to say. In the space of three days one year art assassins brutalized two of the world's greatest works of art. While a group of school children watched in horror, a young man plunged a knife into a seventeenth-century Poussin at the National Gallery in London. Two days later a young Dutchman knifed Van Gogh's *La Berceuse* in Amsterdam's Municipal Museum. Rembrandt's *Night Watch* was slashed thirteen times with a bread knife and Marcel Duchamp's *Network of Stoppages* was also attacked. The usual weapon of the art assassin is a knife. But a hammer was used on the *Pieta* of Michelangelo, and Picasso's *Guernica* was attacked with spray paint . . . they'll use anything: acid, umbrellas — anything."

"You're saying these people are mad?"

"Mostly. There's usually a history of mental illness. They say crazy things like, 'Voices made me do it' or 'I'm Jesus Christ' or 'Kill lies all.' "

"So what you're saying, in effect, is that some loony who'd read about the Seraphine-Olympia" (even the detectives called it that with easy and somewhat affectionate familiarity), "and about the murder of the sitter herself and the roses scattered around, decided to duplicate the act?"

"I'm saying it's possible. Historically there's plenty of precedent in the art world. These people are usually described as being very dazed, or acting strangely. Some are disgruntled artists, but not all by any means — there have been shoemakers, cooks, teachers, geologists, even sailors."

They shook their heads and looked dazed themselves.

"It's a strange world you live in. Do you know of any certified art lunatics who might have done something like this?"

Gregor and I thought furiously. Then we shook our heads in unison. "Not really. The gallery has never had such an episode."

"O.K. Well, we'll continue to look into it. And we'll send the fingerprint boys over for a look, just in case. But I doubt they'll find anything. Meanwhile, leave everything just as it is. The police photographer will be along." And they went off, saying no more and looking inscrutable.

Gregor got out the sherry and poured it with a trembling hand. "I may not live through this, Persis."

"Seraphine already hasn't, Gregor. One at a time. It's not your turn."

"Well, it's certainly not *yours* — I couldn't spare you." That was a big compliment coming from the charming man with the fragile ego who most of the time didn't know I was alive. "Tell me honestly, do you really think it was what you call an art assassin inspired by all the publicity about Seraphine?"

My beloved employer needed to be reassured. He'd had quite enough trouble for one day — he would have said for one lifetime. So I lied.

In truth I wasn't at all sure it was the work of an art assassin, no more than I thought it was the work of Gregor himself.

A lunatic, perhaps. But in that case, the work of the same lunatic who had murdered Seraphine Braceley. Somebody was toying with us, laying paper trails that were not what they seemed, clouding the mirror to obscure the real image, covering the true canvas with the false.

And more than ever, Seraphine needed an alibi.

Chapter 18

Dan Brodsk, Sandy's batman, assistant, and general factotum, had grown into a tall, fine-looking young man, a far cry from the terrified thirteen-year-old I'd seen struggling with Dehorter the night of the power mower death.

He greeted me personally at the gate to Sandy's compound. The gate was locked and I had to follow the posted instructions to ring a bell and announce myself into a sort of grill before he appeared and pushed the right things to open the electronic gate.

He smiled apologetically. "Sorry about this, Mrs. Willum. But with a fortune in paintings on the place, we have to take precautions. You may leave your car here — it's just a few steps."

"I remember."

I remembered, too, that Dan had been brought up here. His mother had been Sandy's housekeeper forever and she and her son guarded the great man fiercely: no other permanent help was allowed on the place. Of course it was wonderful for Sandy to have two such devoted people taking care of his every need. He often said that thanks to them he never had to think of anything but his painting, and that they were worth a household full of servants. Though I don't suppose you could exactly classify Dan Brodsk as a servant — he had too much responsibility for that. He handled all of Sandy's business affairs, and despite his youth, he seemed to do a good job of it.

Looking at Dan now, as he led me across the courtyard to Sandy's studio, I couldn't help thinking of the little boy of so many years ago, struggling to save his patron from Dehorter's fury. Today he was a young man, eyes shaded by fashionable aviator's glasses, brown hair cut very à la mode, smart tie, shirt, jacket, the works. All he needed was a briefcase to play the successful young executive.

I liked him. I liked all young people.

"Has Sandy been working?" I asked.

"Not much lately." His tone was hushed, as if the sacred genius could hear him from the studio a few steps ahead, the studio that had once been a simple, Gull Harbor-type stable, which Sandy had converted by installing central heating, air conditioning, and huge skylights. I remembered that he'd changed the box stalls into storage space, a kitchen, and a bedroom. He'd then finished the "shedrow" walkway by enclosing it, too, in glass. Bamboo shutters controlled the light throughout and I remembered that there had always been green plants and flowers everywhere.

The studio door was shut to signify that Sandy was working. But I knew the ploy — Sandy always rushed to shut it whenever he heard a car drive up. He would be peering out at us now from behind a small one-way glass window set in the wall next to the door. In many ways, Sandy Corsini was still a child.

I was right. The door opened immediately and Sandy was sweeping me up in a big bear hug that might, or might not, be brotherly, depending on one's mood and interpretation.

"Persis, my beauty — it's been weeks. I'd forgotten how gorgeous you are."

"Days, Sandy, actually. The Collectors' Choice preview."

He was dragging me along the corridor that passed what had once been the roomy box stalls, former home of generations of well-bred polo ponies and hunters. I glimpsed a small kitchen, several storerooms, and a bedroom with an oversize bed covered in the skin of some deceased African animal.

The bedroom had a comfortable, used look and I was reminded of an interview I'd once read in *Playboy* in which Sandy declared that he'd had his first sexual encounter at twelve and that, like Guy de Maupassant, he believed a man should have at least three hundred sexual encounters before he was forty. Everyone in Gull Harbor had had a good laugh over that one, chalking it up to artistic bombast.

He was wearing a dark blue wool beret and white shorts — no shoes. Black eyes peered out at me from under bushy black brows.

He embraced me again. "When are you going to pose for me, Little One? I've asked you a hundred times."

"When you're less dangerous," I replied.

"What do you mean? I'm just a simple country boy. Isn't that so, Danny?" It was an old game — he'd been playing it for years. Brodsk looked embarrassed, although he ought to have been used to it by now.

We were in the "visitor's" room, an alcove in the big studio that housed two green velvet sofas and a large studio easel for showing paintings. The working part of the studio was partially hidden by two screens Sandy had painted early in his career and never consented to sell. They featured ravishing tropical birds hidden in lush greenery.

He sat me down on one of the deep plush sofas. I knew from the past that, once seated, it was difficult to extricate oneself from their velvet clutches — all part of the strategy to make it impossible for a collector to escape the studio without a Corsini at a price he later couldn't believe he'd paid.

Today he was being Picasso — bare, brown, fuzzy torso and all.

"You've heard about the painting, Sandy?"

"Gregor called me. And the police, wanting to know if I had any theories."

"Do you?"

He laughed. "None at all, although I might have done it myself if it weren't my own work. That Seraphine!"

"Did she steal the *Olympia*, Sandy?"

"Damn well did. Decamped with it while I was in Chicago with Brodsk overseeing the installation of a major show of my work. No word of warning — just took off. Left a note. Never saw her again."

"What kind of note?"

He laughed once more, a genuine, hearty guffaw without malice. "It was typical Seraphine. I framed it to remind me never to marry again. Here, I'll show you." He got up with surprising agility from the sofa where he'd installed himself beside me and stepped around the screens. I heard his heavy footsteps cross the floor. Then he was back, holding a framed piece of paper.

He handed it to me. "Here. See for yourself."

What I read was "Received of Sandro

Corsini in full recompense for one year's service as his legal wife." She'd signed it in a mad flourish of curves and letters.

It was a ridiculous document. I suppose she'd kept a copy. But what did it mean legally? "Didn't you try to get her back — if not Seraphine, surely the painting? It had already cost you so much."

Sandy was a canny peasant, the last man to let anyone steal from him. He'd be the first to pursue what was his. And he'd know how to do it — he had the money to hire the people who could.

He shrugged. "I didn't want to make a fuss. And you know how it is . . . it's the women around here who make or break a fellow. Didn't want to antagonize them by seeming to be mean to Seraphine. The men know nothing about art — they buy what their wives tell them to buy. All the men understand is the bottom line. I couldn't afford to offend the ladies."

What he was saying had a certain truth. The women had made Sandy a social success long before he married Seraphine. He was invited everywhere. And after Seraphine left, they'd seen to it that he continued to be the catch of every season.

While his prices went up and up.

He took up his station beside me and

leaned forward. "Lovely girl," he said, "all that was long ago. This is now and you're here and I'm so happy." He said it like a caress, his smile baring large, perfect, white teeth, animal magnetism leaking out of every pore.

I smiled back, hoping the sunlight streaming mercilessly in on me didn't reveal every thirty-seven-year-old flaw to the master. "You mentioned tea, Sandy."

"Did I? I would have walked barefoot to Damascus to get you here — don't you know that?"

Brodsk had returned and was standing in the doorway. Sandy noticed him for the first time. "Oh, Danny, how about some tea for Mrs. Willum?"

"Sure." Brodsk didn't smile as he left.

"Fine boy," Sandy said. "But absolutely no sense of timing. I think he believes I'll go straight to hell if he doesn't watch me every minute."

He gave his lusty ha-ha-ha and laid a heavy bare arm along the back of the sofa. He smelled faintly of something crisp and attractively male and I squirmed cautiously forward away from his arm. I wasn't used to bare men so close to me at this hour.

One thigh touched mine. Dangerous black eyes burned into mine. I tried to draw away as tactfully as possible. "It's too early in the day for this, Sandro."

But he had laced his fingers in my hair and he drew my head back. His free hand began to caress my body. "Carissima ... I've always wanted you since the first time I saw you."

One of my earrings came off and dropped onto the cushion between us. "Stop, Sandy." It was undignified, embarrassing.

Rather to my surprise, he stopped instantly. "I'm sorry. But you're charming, you know. I can't be blamed. Let me paint you. May I?"

I felt around until I found my earring and clipped it on. I straightened my blouse. My skirt. He watched all this with amusement, his arm still across the back of the sofa, his fingers still tangled in my hair, his bare torso searingly close.

It was a blatantly, outrageously sexy performance.

"You're playing the silent movie villain, Sandro Corsini. How can I take you seriously?"

"Try me. Let me paint you. Then you'll find out. You won't be sorry." The banked passion with which he said these ordinary words gave them new meaning.

Dan Brodsk came into the studio alcove just then. If he noticed the tension, he didn't betray it. "My mother is here with the tea," he said loudly, as if speaking to deaf people.

The rattling of china heralded the arrival of the housekeeper.

Sandy disengaged his fingers and changed the angle of his body. The moment had passed.

"Ah, Mrs. Brodsk, how nice. Little sandwiches? I could eat a horse after working all day. Persis, will you pour? I never thought the day would come when I'd be drinking tea in the afternoon — my peasant ancestors would die laughing. But there must be some English blood in me somewhere, because I love it. That's fine, Mrs. Brodsk, thank you. Danny, would you show Mrs. Willum the new work?"

For the next hour we sipped tea while Dan Brodsk brought out painting after painting. Most of them were works Sandy wouldn't sell. Like Picasso, he only released a few paintings at a time; the rest were reserved for his own collection and for museums.

Seraphine's name wasn't mentioned again until just before I left, when the artist remarked casually, "So you've just come from Amsterdam, I hear. I may have a show there one day. What do you think of the town?"

I told him I liked it.

"And did you hear anything about Seraphine? Meet anyone who knew her? She was living there, you know. Did you learn anything?"

So that was it. This whole afternoon had been about Amsterdam. "How did you know I was there?"

"Everybody knows. That's Gull Harbor. Did you hear anything?"

"No," I said. "Not one thing."

After that he was quite willing to let me go.

Constanza Brodsk was waiting to do the honors at the gate.

I'd encountered her numerous times before today, but I'd never really noticed her. She was always a figure in the background, serving meals, taking guests' coats and making them disappear, moving swiftly and self-effacingly. Everyone in Gull Harbor knew that she and her son had been with Sandy since his wife's suicide — probably before — we didn't really know him before. I'd heard it said by someone that she ruled Sandy's compound with an iron hand and was completely dedicated to him in the manner of an old-world slave to its master. It was generally assumed because of her name that she was a refugee from some Balkan country; but she had no accent to prove or disprove the theory.

Looking at her now in the full sunlight I saw that she was a broad-cheeked woman with traces of beauty. If I'd been asked, I would have compared her to one of the bathers in Renoir's later paintings. But perhaps that was the artist in me, always looking for something special.

She spoke to me now for the very first time that I could recall, other than the occasional "thank you, ma'am" we'd all heard a million times.

"Excuse me, but may I speak? My son tells me that you are very kind. I don't know where to turn. Could you help me — advise me?"

What could this be about? I paused uneasily and leaned against my open car door. "You have a fine son, Mrs. Brodsk."

"I thank you. He has always been a good boy." She paused and looked away. "I have nothing to complain about. Not until now. That is why I wanted to speak to you."

I sensed trouble and wished I could escape. The last thing I wanted was to get into the middle of a quarrel between Sandy and his people. And it sounded like that was what was coming. "Perhaps Mr. Corsini could help you."

But that wasn't what she wanted. In fact she looked behind her nervously to see if anyone was watching. There was a long pause, then she went on. "It's the company he keeps. He doesn't come home at night — sometimes he is gone for several days. He says it's business for Mr.

Corsini, but I don't believe it. I think it's a woman. Because he is different. Not my boy any longer. He doesn't tell me who his friends are. He likes you, Mrs. Willum. If you could talk to him . . ."

"But Mrs. Brodsk . . ."

"Another thing — he's trying to change his name. Brodsk isn't good enough for him any more. I found letters — Daniel Broadman. And when I faced him with it, he told me he's an American and Brodsk is not an American name."

"But that's not serious. Many Americans of European descent change their names."

"It's those women. They're after him. He wants to be like them. Always asking about his father . . . who was he . . . when did he die . . . where are we from . . . it's those women."

It sounded normal enough to me. I didn't blame him. "His father is dead?"

"Yes." Nothing further.

"Well, he's an attractive young man, Mrs. Brodsk. He's feeling his oats."

"But not with these women. They will destroy him."

"How old is your son, Mrs. Brodsk?"

"Twenty-three."

"Then he's no longer a child. He is only being an American young man — trying to spread his wings, growing up, being independent. It's to be expected. Don't worry."

But she wasn't consoled. "You're out there in the world, Mrs. Willum. You're what they call a career woman. If you could warn him . . . tell him to watch out for bad company. Mr. Corsini is an artist. Artists are impractical about the ways of the world. So he would just laugh at me."

I didn't disillusion her by pointing out that I, too, was an artist. "But your son is a fine young man. He is handling Mr. Corsini's affairs, and that is a very important job. He has a lot of responsibility for his age. He has to play now and then. It's normal, at his age."

"I understand that. And he pretends that Mr. Corsini even sent him to organize an exhibition in his first wife's gallery — they both pretend. But I don't believe it — he's unhappy and troubled. If you could . . ." Two red spots of color now glowed in her cheeks and she really did look Renoiresque. But it wasn't her looks that made me straighten up and pay attention. ". . . what was that? Mr. Corsini's first wife? I thought she was dead? I thought she committed suicide?"

"Oh, no, Mrs. Willum. She tried once to kill herself, but she didn't succeed. Slit her wrists; but he came home and found her before much damage was done except to the bathroom and bedroom rugs. She was too nice — not tough enough. He pushed her around; a man despises a woman he can push around. So in the end she left. It was better for both of them."

"But I always understood . . ."

"Of course. It was easier that way. Everybody was sorry for him. A man like him — a woman doesn't leave a man like him." There was something mocking about the way she said it.

I leaned against the car and stared at her, wondering if she was sincere or if she was playing a game with me. And while I was standing there she thanked me as profusely as if I had already rescued her son from a life of sin, and went away.

I didn't even have the wit to ask her the name of Sandy's first wife, nor the name and location of her gallery. But it didn't matter. I already knew.

The only thing I didn't know was whether Sandy's housekeeper had really wanted me to help her son — it seemed absurd on the face of it . . . or if the whole thing had been an excuse to tell me exactly what she'd told me.

I just didn't know for sure . . .

Chapter 19

All the way over to Etienne Dehorter's house, Locusts, the image of Dan Brodsk and his mother kept haunting me. That nice young man — a boy who had grown up in his master's world until now he belonged in that world more than in his mother's ... no wonder she was disturbed; she had the old-fashioned idea of a servant's proper place. I'd seen it happen before in Gull Harbor when servants became their employer's confidants and seconds-in-command. Sometimes they graduated into private secretaries, hunting companions, tennis partners, trainers of their master's racing stables, and even associates in business. The old barriers were falling; and what serving class there remained was expected to be better educated, capable of handling a wide variety of matters formerly dealt with by the employer or his wife, and to demand and get high salaries, good living quarters, and cars.

Brodsk was such a new nonservant, obviously. He was capable not only of serving the champagne, but also of arranging the artist's appointment book, filtering the visitors, negotiating his exhibition schedules, and dealing with museums and galleries world-wide. Sandy had trained him for this job from youth and couldn't be better served than by a young man who knew everything there was to know about the Master Painter and was as loyal as his own son.

Constanza Brodsk was another matter. While she did not particularly look like a servant — she had been dressed in simple print blouse and dark skirt — my impression had been that she was disturbed, not by her son's seeing women, but *certain* women; and the only kind of women Constanza Brodsk, the faithful, old-fashioned servant, would have been disturbed about were what she thought of as women outside of his class. Gull Harbor women, for example. And she would have been disturbed with good reason: Gull Harbor women were notorious man-eaters, voracious and heartless and relentless in pursuit of their prey. Their preference was for young, unspoiled fellows . . . schoolboy sons of their friends . . . skating and tennis pros . . . visiting sailors who crewed on their yachts in summer. Anything young. Anything good-looking. Anything fresh.

So had Constanza really been asking me for

help with her son? It was Sandy's job, not mine. Had she told me about Sandy's first wife to remind me that Sandy couldn't be trusted with the truth? Or was she trying to buy my cooperation by offering me a tidbit of information generally unknown in Gull Harbor?

Could the whole scene have been staged? But if so — why?

And how did everybody know I'd been in Amsterdam? Had Gregor broadcast the news to assure the collectors that he was doing everything humanly possible to find Seraphine and resolve the problem of the notorious *Olympia?* It would be like him.

Beginning with Withers, who had arranged the tickets, the whole of Gull Harbor and environs must have known I was there. And the whole of Gull Harbor might now know everything I knew.

Whatever that was.

But if the purpose of her speaking to me had actually been to reveal that Sandy's first wife was alive — why had she done that? And why tell *me?*

The whole afternoon had been a series of why's. And I couldn't answer any of them.

I pulled over to the side of the road and checked my mirror before starting up the half mile locust-lined driveway to Etienne Dehorter's. I refreshed my lipstick — most of it had melted away with Sandy's tea. I tried to tame the disorder of my blondish hair. I even dabbed a touch of Dior on my ears.

Why did I care about being perfect when I visited Dehorter? Maybe it was because I'd just come from Seraphine's second husband, who had found me attractive enough to muss me up, and I didn't want to give Dehorter ideas by arriving looking like I'd just come from a romp in the hay. Not that he'd be likely to have ideas — not even if I walked in stark naked. He was a cold one. Nevertheless, I fussed and poked and primped until I thought there was an improvement; only then did I zoom down his drive and into his turnaround.

A red Ferrari was parked at the front door. The license plate read "POLO." A blue Mercedes coupe was parked next to it.

A dignified major-domo, who was new to me, ushered me into a pale blue drawing room, its modest color taking care not to detract from the priceless Chippendale furniture gleaming darkly under great gilt mirrors and the violent Expressionist paintings Dehorter was now collecting. In this one room alone I saw a work by the Norwegian Edvard Munch, whose intensity of emotion channeled into his painting had led to an eventual breakdown. There was an Ensor, the Belgian precursor of Expressionism who lived in solitude all his life — this canvas a big oil and crayon featuring disturbing masked figures.

There was a tortured Rouault Christ in blood reds and black. Soutine was there, represented by a characteristic twitching landscape executed in twisting, thrashing strokes of red and green.

Each painting was a major example of the artist's work. Each was unsettling and disturbing and the farthest possible cry from the Impressionist collection now permanently residing in the Dehorter wing of the Waldheim. For miraculously, despite the brouhaha of the night of Pinky's party and the Body on the Power Mower and the fisticuffs over the painting of Seraphine that had been originally destined to grace the wing, Etienne Dehorter had kept his word. The funds were donated. The wing was built. The paintings were installed. Only the notorious *Olympia* was missing.

And now, like its subject, it had been murdered.

I found Dehorter's "second" collection extremely disturbing. In Seraphine's day, the atmosphere of this room had been warm and casual and welcoming. The new collection changed all that. The angry, turbulent, often violent feeling of the work left me agitated and uneasy. I wondered how Dehorter could live with these paintings, which must be scattered all through his house. These furious canvases peering down from the walls were as intimidating as the collector himself.

Dehorter let me sit and stare at them for a while. He himself didn't consent to appear for about ten minutes.

He was wearing an old shooting jacket with his usual faultless elegance. I could never get over how attractive he could be in a withdrawn sort of way, even at this age. Maybe what I found intriguing was the invisible "don't touch" sign he wore. It was the same chilling look of hauteur that the French aristocracy had worn on the way to the guillotine.

"You're looking well, Persis." The way he said it, I wondered if he'd ever seen me before. Probably not, considering the magnificent view his wife had given from all sides.

"You're very kind. Gregor wants you to know that he's sorry about the other night. He never would have unwrapped the painting at the opening if he'd known — he'd never have embarrassed you. But he thought it was me for a drink. "What will it be? Champagne? I seem to recall being told that champagne is your drink. Moët suit you?"

"Perfectly, thank you."

He gave the butler his marching orders. I noticed that he himself ordered Perrier — no wonder he was so fit. We chitchatted back and forth until the drinks arrived and were served, mine in a beautiful antique, etched-glass flute.

Then Dehorter got down to business.

"So you've been in Amsterdam." It wasn't a question: he was stating a fact.

Had I hired a town crier unbeknownst to myself to spread the news? Was *everyone* interested in my trip? It began to look that way.

"Business." You could say so.

"I understand my ex-wife was living there just before her death."

"So I've been told. Naturally, I didn't see her."

"But you must have tried to look her up, talked to her friends." He spoke off-handedly, sipping his Perrier and gazing around the room at his paintings as if he were just making polite conversation and the whole matter held no real interest for him.

I stared at him woodenly to let him know that the conversation had no interest for me either. "No," I said.

"Ah, well." He worked on the cigarette again, fitting it deeper into the holder. "Weren't you a little bit surprised that she'd insist on sending something for the Collectors' Choice when you knew she couldn't possibly have anything worthy of being included?"

I explained a little about the phone call. "You know how impulsive she was. I even wondered, frankly, if you could have given her something worthwhile in the divorce settlement."

He yanked out the cigarette, crumpled it up, and threw it into a scrap basket. "Have you heard of fat chance? She left *me*, if you recall."

That was when Christine Kelley spoke. Her entrance on bare feet was so silent that she could have been standing in the doorway for minutes before we were aware of her. She was wearing something silk and Chinese and slit up the side nearly to her waist. Her exposed brown leg and tightly wrapped little muscular body would have turned any man's head except Dehorter's — there wasn't a flicker of lust in his cool eyes. In fact, he barely glanced at her.

"What are you quizzing Persis about, Darling?" She moved swiftly across the room and perched on his knees, one slender tanned arm around his neck, her other hand caressing his chest. Her body language was announcing that this was *her* territory and that she intended to defend it.

"I had such a lovely nap," she went on, making it clear that not only Dehorter but his bed, too, belonged to her.

What could this be? Surely she wasn't jealous of me — I'd never given Dehorter a sideways glance. It had to be Seraphine. Even dead, she stirred jealousy in the survivors.

Christine's fingers now moved to the back of his neck and she ran them lightly up and down in a gesture frankly meant to arouse him.

But he was unmoved. "Why are you so interested?" he asked coldly.

"Because everything about you interests me." And she tried to kiss him; but he stood up, almost dumping her on the rug. "Don't you have something to do?" And he all but pushed her out of the room.

I didn't like Christine Kelley — never had. She was a tough little thing, still out to land a rich man, without notable success to date. Apparently no one rich enough to suit her had offered matrimony. Dehorter was obviously the present target. It was a desperately serious business for her; in a year or two she'd be too old either to go on riding races or to catch a millionaire. She'd taken up polo to get this one and she was determined to land him.

When she had retreated, he tried once more. "Did Seraphine mention Christine when she called about the painting?"

I was astonished. "Why, no. Why would she?"

"Well, then." He managed a wintery smile. "Thanks so much for coming by. It was nice of you. It's been too long."

The interview was finished. What had it been about, anyway? Whether I'd found out something about Seraphine in Amsterdam? What else could it be?

Or did it have to do with Christine Kelley, and if so, what was her connection with Seraphine?

I crawled into my little Mustang shaking my head in bafflement.

Chapter 20

Pinky was giving another party. I'd almost forgotten in the shock of Seraphine's murder. A note from Mrs. Howard reminded me.

As usual, it was pinned to Isadore Duncan's dinner with instructions.

"Don't forget Isadore's cream chicken," it ordered. "Warm and feed before departure."

It took me a minute to figure out whose departure. Mrs. Howard's? Isadore's? Or, most alarming of all, mine?

Then, luckily, I remembered Pinky's party — a dance this time, in honor of their anniversary. Seraphine's death was not about to disrupt this great social affair; after all, it wasn't Pinky's or his wife's fault that Seraphine had had the poor taste to get herself murdered.

The dance would go on as planned. Seraphine had caused quite enough disruptions.

Pinky had taken over the Gull Harbor club for the occasion. Cocktails would be served downstairs; dinner and dancing would be observed in the walnut-paneled upstairs dining room. There would be about a hundred and twenty guests, Gregor had said.

There was just time to call Simms before Gregor, who was to be my date, came to fetch me with his car and driver.

This time he was not in his office . . . his answering machine was manning the fort instead.

I'm thrilled to talk to answering machines. Since I hate telephones almost as much as Isadore Duncan does, I'm delighted to leave messages all over the place, knowing they will save me another phone call.

This message was brief.

"Listen, Ed, it's Persis. What about all those ne'er-do-well husbands Seraphine married after Corsini? Three, weren't there? Could one of them have killed her?"

Then I fed Isadore her perfectly warmed chicken à la crème, adding a dollop of white wine for good measure, and scrounged around in my closet for something respectable to wear among the dispirited rags that hung there. Isadore took two licks of her dinner and then stalked in to supervise. I settled for a bias-cut putty-colored crepe that belied its age and mine. "O.K.?" I demanded of my feline audience of one. She didn't deign to answer. So I whipped my hair into some semblance of order, splashed a dash of eyeliner around my eyes to bring out their gray, flung on some lipstick, and called it a wrap.

"Not too bad?" I asked Isadore hopefully.

She frowned and stalked out of the room: she'd heard Gregor's car in the drive.

"Don't wait up for me," I told her.

Isadore wasn't amused; she hates spending the evening alone, even if I leave the TV on for company. So she put up her tail stiff as a flagpole and marched furiously into the kitchen. I felt sorry for anyone who might have the temerity to telephone that evening — she would certainly knock the phone off the hook.

All the men were in black tie and at first glance the club looked as if it were hosting a conference of penguins. But then the ladies and their dashes of color burst out of the black in brilliant Fauve splashes, like accents on a dark-primed canvas.

If I knew anything about couture, I would probably have been able to identify each world-class designer represented here tonight and even quote prices. But as I'm a starving artist and thus clearly unable to afford the designer game, I'd long ago decided to rise above the whole thing and stick to the precept that ignorance is bliss. Gregor never minded the way I looked, so I couldn't be missing much.

And sure enough, "You look smashing, Persis," he said as he steered me though the cocktail crowd. "These women are all overdressed."

They didn't look overdressed to me: they looked wonderful. Most of them were gathered around Sandro Corsini like a bouquet of flowers. Betsy Smith was in pale pink satin that complemented her fragile fairness, Angela Roth was in dark green chiffon and emeralds to show off her black eyes and hair, Tinka Wheeler was in red silk that complemented her milk-white skin, Marianna McCoy had chosen dove gray embroidered with seed pearls, and Christine Kelley wore a black top over a billowing flower-printed taffeta skirt. Sam Swann was in ice blue to set off her red hair. Even Jordan Braceley's wife Missy was there, gazing adoringly at Sandy. She was the only one in a short dress, her black velvet, tulip-shaped skirt skimming neat, rounded knees. Apparently she had forsworn her "going to ground" for this one big event.

It was always like that — they all paid court to Sandy. All of them, at one time or another, had been invited to sit for figures in his weirdly unfathomable dreamscapes and they loved knowing that they were in the museums and great exhibitions, captured for posterity among the formal, fully clothed, stiffly staring figures seated in cafés where waiters would never serve them, walking through railway stations where trains would never come, strolling down streets that never were. Though no face was ever fully recognizable, they knew they were *there* and that they had actually worn such and such a meticulously painted dress or hat or coat, now perhaps discarded but preserved on Corsini's canvas. They were part of it and they bragged to one another and to all the matrons who hadn't been so honored.

"I'm in *Dreamscape Number Eleven.*"

"Well, I'm in *August Moon Four.*"

"You'll find me in the station of *The Last Train.*"

These were the not-quite-middle-aged women who made Gull Harbor society, and decided who else would make it or not.

And they had decreed that Sandro Corsini was the greatest social lion on the social scene. No important party was a success without him. His presence was guaranteed to make or break a party.

"There's Sandy," Gregor, jealous as always of the attention Corsini generated, said crossly. "As usual, the women are falling all over him. I guess that means Pinky's party is made."

I thought of Pinky's most memorable party.

"At least he isn't late." Sandy and Gregor were Gull Harbor's two notorious latecomers. I noticed Dan Brodsk stationed at Sandy's side like the faithful lieutenant he was. His mother was right, he didn't look particularly happy.

Seeing him reminded me. "Do you remember the Body on the Power Mower? Whatever came of all that, I wonder?"

"I'd almost forgotten," Gregor answered. "Not much came of it. I talked to the D.A. recently at some function or other. He seems to agree with your theory of the time — she was a stringer looking for material for Francy James's column and she climbed on the power mower to keep from ruining her shoes and somehow drove into a tree branch that she didn't see in the rain. One slight puzzle — they found one of her shoes caught in the library terrace door but they concluded that it didn't mean anything. There was so much confusion with everyone milling around that they think someone found it on the ground and dropped it there." What he was saying, more than anything, was that somebody had bungled.

A white-coated steward came through the room just then, beating a large brass gong and announcing dinner upstairs.

"We've barely had time to have a drink, let alone make the rounds and speak to anyone,"

Gregor complained. He's a sociable soul.

I glanced at the diamond watch my aunt had given me. "That's because you were late. You're always late, Gregor. I don't even bother getting dressed until half an hour after you're supposed to pick me up." It was true, had always been true. Sometimes, when we traveled abroad on business, he was still in the shower when the plane was scheduled to leave. I'd grown used to it over the years and adjusted my own mental time clock accordingly.

"I'm never late," he told me severely. "Never missed a plane in my life."

"That's because they wait," I answered. "Come on. When the dancing starts they'll forget all about Sandy Corsini, because he's clumsy as a bear. They'll be swarming all over you, Gregor."

"That's right." He smiled happily and began to hustle me upstairs. Sandy and his bouquet of human flowers moved along ahead of us, trailed by the faithful Dan Brodsk. Gregor was humming happily to himself, imagining the moment when dinner would finally be over and he could sweep me out onto the dance floor for a bit of Rogers and Astaire while Gull Harbor's make-or-break hostesses looked on and waited impatiently for him to finish with me so it could be their turn.

I, on the other hand, was imagining a shoe

. . . a single one, dropped in a doorway on a rainy night.

Dinner went the way Gull Harbor dinners usually go. The women flirt. The men tend to ignore them and bolt down the superb food and drinks without tasting anything. In this case, it was a creamy soup with white wine, a perfect filet of beef in tarragon butter with a garnish of perfectly steamed vegetables served with a good Burgundy, followed by a confection of fruit and cream and champagne. I seriously believe Gull Harbor men consider talking to women a waste of time, unless they're talking them into bed, which is another matter.

Some of the best men were at my table — Randy McCoy, Towny Smith, and Howard Roth. I'd hoped with such a talented array that the conversation would include the ladies for once. But it was a vain hope; as usual they mostly talked to one another — "woman talk" bored them stiff. When the music started, things would be better: they loved having their arms around women other than their wives and on the dance floor it was perfectly legal. Furthermore, it was the perfect place to try to drum up an assignation.

But for now, these tycoons had time only for each other; while the ladies looked around at the other guests and gossiped back and forth across the table.

Tinka Wheeler was talking about a trip to the Bahamas.

At the same time Christine Kelley was talking about a polo game in Deauville.

Then suddenly the name of Pieter Joosten was heard and everybody at the table, women included, shut up and paid attention.

". . . can't quote my sources, naturally, but I've got it on good authority that it's true. Poor devil," Howard Roth said.

"Good authority meaning your own people?" Randall McCoy, not laughing.

"Well, it's no secret from you fellows that our pharmaceutical division is concentrating on a cure for AIDS. Isn't everybody? We're even cooperating with Amsterdam and Paris on it. That's where the future lies. You're all heavily invested, one way or another, so don't pretend you don't know."

They nodded.

"And you're saying Joosten was researching . . ."

"You've got it. Brilliant fellow — scientist, researcher, metallurgist . . . anything at all where there was a challenge. You've all met the type — some great things have come out of men like that. Did some interesting work in the field of metallurgy on new, nonflammable materials for aircraft bodies, for example, that didn't pan out. Not practical. Zeroed in on AIDS when the AIDS thing began. Kind of guy who couldn't resist a challenge."

Towny Smith broke in. "Didn't he address that conference in Brussels we all attended? Weren't the reps of all the aircraft companies there?"

"That's where we first got to talking," Roth admitted. "Invited him here to talk airplane materials, but it was just a ruse. It was his AIDS work that really interested us."

The ladies had abandoned their gossip. "But he never arrived," one of them said. "What happened? You know, don't you."

Howard Roth signaled the waiter to replenish the wineglasses. "When he didn't show, we sent out all the bird dogs we could muster and the scent led them to . . ." He paused to sip his wine and to heighten the suspense.

"To where?" the ladies cried in unison. "Don't tease us. Howard."

"To a clinic in Amsterdam," he answered finally. "He was registered there under an assumed name, which was why nobody found him earlier."

"An assumed name? But *why?*"

"Because he'd come down with AIDS, that's why. Because nobody wants the world to know they have the disease, that's also why. Poor devil. Was it his research? Or was it the fast life in Amsterdam? He wasn't married, after all. We'll never know."

There was silence as the full implication hit us.

"Claimed he notified Harrington House that he was ill and couldn't come," Roth continued. "But we never got the message. And here we were, checkbooks open, hoping he'd turn up with a formula we could buy. The metallurgy thing was just a cover — we didn't want the competition sniffing around."

"You mean he was never here at all?" Tinka was pink with excitement.

"So it would appear."

"Dying, I suppose," Christine Kelley said without noticeable sympathy. "So much for the free and easy life."

It seemed to me she should be the last to criticize.

"I suppose the police know?" McCoy wasn't really asking.

"Of course. May have known for quite some time, in fact."

We were all bemused.

"Then who was the messenger?" someone asked.

"Who indeed?"

I looked around the table at them all. They weren't paying the least attention to anyone but Howard Roth, their eyes locked in on him, their faces closed and expressionless.

To the rest of the room we all probably looked perfectly normal. But we weren't.

Because somebody at Harrington House must have known Joosten wasn't coming.

And I thought — every important man in Gull Harbor is on the board of Harrington House.

They all could have known.

The rest of the night stuck to the script. When dinner was over, Gregor came from wherever he had been sitting to ask first his hostess, then me for a dance.

Gregor is a marvelous dancer. The music is born in him: he can anticipate a beat before it happens. He not only moves with the music, he enhances and glorifies it. It's an honor to dance with him, to be carried away in his arms.

I personally believe that good dancers are made in heaven. It's not something you can learn, like typing or computer arts. Dancing is a gift — like painting.

And Gregor, who can't play the piano or any other musical instrument, is transformed at the first note the orchestra strikes up. He knows the next note before they do.

So we did our number, and when it was over he moved on to Angela and Betsy and

Missy and Tinka and Marianna McCoy and Sam Swann and finished up by whirling Christine Kelley and even Lily Armbruster around the floor in a grand finale.

While this was going on I wasn't exactly a wallflower. They all danced with me. And I loved every minute. In fact, there were even one or two propositions I might seriously have considered, now that I had finally once and for all given Oliver Reynolds, my ubiquitous suitor, his walking papers. Ultimately the moment arrived when it was imperative to repair my lipstick and the ravages to my hair from a dozen perspiring male faces pressed ardently down on the top of it.

The "loo," as it's debonairly known in Gull Harbor, is approximately the size of Yankee Stadium. There is one room with banks of mirrors and dressing tables and one wall of full-length mirrors, and a second room with a half-dozen showers, in case it should come into your head to take one in the middle of a dance, and also about six of the usual amenities.

When I arrived to attend to the vital repairs and seated myself at one of the dressing tables, peering discouragedly into the minor at the wreck of what had earlier been the moderately glamorous Persis Willum, I heard low voices coming from the room behind me. The door was closed, but it didn't matter . . . clearly the leaders of Gull Harbor society were having an informal caucus.

"I suppose you all know about Joosten, don't you?"

"What about him?"

"He couldn't have been the messenger. Howard's known it all along — maybe they all have . . . they're all on Harrington's board. Harrington House got word at the last minute saying he couldn't come."

"Why not?"

"AIDS, my dear. And are you surprised? Remember when we all went to Amsterdam after the Brussels conference?" There was an outburst of giggles.

"And after the conference at The Hague," somebody added.

"Well, you know Amsterdam. Dinner at the Osterbar — then the sex shows. Funny, all those proper business types in the audience pretending they're there by mistake. Remember when we were both there last week and . . ." someone said in a near whisper. I didn't quite recognize the voice.

Last week? I wondered if even the police knew that these solid citizens had been in Amsterdam. And at about the time Seraphine Braceley had a rendezvous with a killer.

"So Joosten was a free-liver . . . that's what you're saying?"

"That's what *Howard's* saying. I'll bet he's known all along. But it took a while, because Joosten entered a sanatorium under an assumed name. Even in Amsterdam, they're beginning to be afraid of the disease."

"Why didn't someone . . ."

". . . tell about it?" There was a laugh — a trio of trilling silver notes like three silver stilettos. "They wanted to verify it . . . had to track him down under the assumed name, naturally."

"Naturally," they all chorused. Then they changed the subject.

The same old question was dancing around in my head. If the unfortunate Joosten wasn't the messenger — who was? And what had become of him?

And what about Gull Harbor's most formidable tycoons and their wives?

No wonder the whole town knew I had been in Amsterdam . . . they'd all been there, too. And not exactly strictly on business.

I went thoughtfully back downstairs. I didn't want the ladies to emerge from their caucus and find me listening. They wouldn't have liked my knowing.

Definitely not.

Chapter 21

The light on my answering machine was blinking when Gregor delivered me to my house about two A.M. The message was from Ed Simms, who informed me that all of Seraphine's interim husbands had airtight alibis and couldn't possibly be implicated.

I was dead tired. But it wasn't from dancing, although my scale said I'd danced off four never-to-be-mourned pounds.

It was all those rotten questions — the ones that wouldn't go away and wouldn't let me sleep. Maybe if I could get it down on paper, I could also get it all off my mind and spend the few hours that remained before it was time to rise and shine again in fruitful and blissful sleep.

So I sat up in bed with Isadore draped like a ton of bricks across my feet purring enthusiastically and began to make a list of the events as I saw them. It made me feel efficient and in control. It also gave me something to do.

1. Seraphine Braceley was determined to

send us a painting and hinted that it would cause a sensation and embarrass her two first husbands.

2. She gave it to a man she had just met who claimed to be Dr. Pieter Joosten on his way to Gull Harbor.

3. The messenger was supposed to be a scientist about to attend a conference with assembled scientific types at Harrington House.

4. Every important financier and industrialist in Gull Harbor sat on the board of Harrington House and could have had advance knowledge of Joosten's impending visit and of his later cancellation.

5. Seraphine persuaded the supposed Joosten to change his flight. She drove with him to De Gaulle airport in Paris and spent the night with him in Roissy.

6. The next morning she saw to it personally that the painting got aboard the flight to New York.

7. The true Joosten was in an Amsterdam clinic, a victim of AIDS.

8. The false Joosten arrived, checked into Harrington House, deposited his bag and passport in his room, and disappeared.

9. The next day, his car was discovered in the bay.

10. In the middle of the preview, Air France

delivered the painting. It turned out to be the infamous Seraphine *Olympia,* seen now for the first time.

11. Seraphine Braceley was found murdered on the outskirts of De Gaulle airport. The famous Winston Reed diamond was still on her finger.

I sat back against my pillows and stared at my notes, eyes bleary with fatigue. Eleven pieces of a puzzle scattered about at random, waiting for some discerning eye to arrange them in an order that would finally produce a completed picture.

But whose eye?

Not mine. At least not tonight.

I turned out the light and fell asleep. The last thing I remember thinking was that Isadore Duncan's motor ran a lot more smoothly than my Mustang's.

It must have been about five in the morning when Gregor came pounding on my door.

"Persis — Persis . . . wake up . . . let me in."

In the quiet of dignified Gull Harbor, a man shouting on one's doorstep and banging on the front door at five A.M. is guaranteed to get a woman out of bed in a hurry. I was in my robe and unbolting the door even before Isadore Duncan could collect her wits.

I've never seen Gregor look worse.

"What on earth is it, Gregor? Can I get you a drink?"

His hair was every which way and he had crawled into bits and pieces of unmatched clothing, a far cry from the debonair figure he usually presented.

He walked unsteadily over to my bar and poured a large Scotch. "I've been up practically all night. I'd barely gotten home and into bed and asleep when Sandy called and asked me to identify the body. Swore he couldn't do it himself. Said he'd surely fall off the wagon if he did . . . couldn't possibly withstand the emotional strain so would I please — as a favor? I mean, what could I say?"

"Body? What body?"

"Danny Brodsk. Somebody hit him on the head in the parking lot. Planning to rob him, no doubt, or steal the car. Guard came along but not in time. Two or three blows, with something like a baseball bat. Head a bloody mess. Dead as can be. Not my job to do the honors, but Sandy's fallen apart."

"Gregor!"

"Sandy sent him to get the car, remember? We all heard. Sandy never lets anyone else drive his precious old Bentley. When he was slow coming back, Sandy got impatient and sent one of the security guards to find him. Found him, all right."

"Oh, no," I said.

"What? Well, you can imagine the state Sandy's in, not to mention Danny Brodsk himself, of course."

First the Famous Correspondent. Then Seraphine. Then the painting. And now this.

I think I'd been expecting it all along.

Chapter 22

Time was running out.

And there was work to be done, so I started the minute I walked into the North Shore Galleries that morning, ignoring everything else that went on around me.

I began by going through the files and calling every artist I knew who lived in Long Island, Queens, Brooklyn, Manhattan, Connecticut, and New Jersey, which wasn't as many artists as you might imagine because my criterion was income — they had to have a good one. Then I did the same with a select group of collectors.

The question was always the same. "Have you ever put your paintings in a warehouse? If so, which one?"

Mostly, but not always, the answer was "no." It was among certain collectors and the artists who lived in small studio apartments in New York City that I had the best response. Collectors who buy art only for investment are inclined to buy in huge job lots and warehouse the works the way other people deposit money in a bank for safe-keeping. And artists living in very small quarters don't have room to store their work and use warehouses as extra studio space . . . a warehouse is cheaper today than paying for a downtown loft.

It took all day and about three million phone calls, because I followed up on every warehouse mentioned. The question here was also always the same.

"You've heard of Seraphine Braceley, who was killed in Paris? On behalf of the estate, we're trying to track down her collection. Is it stored with you?"

Such was the power of the North Shore Galleries' name and Gregor's reputation as a big-time dealer that nobody asked for further credentials. They all cheerfully called up their records on their computers and said "no." That's the art world for you.

It wasn't until about three in the afternoon that I had any luck. A New Jersey warehouse finally came up affirmative. They'd had the Braceley collection, they told me . . . and to their sorrow. Several years ago a segment of it had been crated and shipped to England. The rest had remained in storage with the bill unpaid. Legal action had been threatened. Summonses had been issued. Papers had pursued Seraphine throughout the world and never been answered. Finally the warehouse had been forced to auction off the paintings remaining in their hands. The revenues from the auction had not covered their expenses. The artists were unknown and unsung and, they told me grimly, actually pretty lousy.

How many paintings had been sent to England? I asked, and what were they.

Forty, they responded. What were they? Nobody knew exactly — they had arrived wrapped and packed in paper cartons in the first place. But the lading sheet listed them as being by more unknowns — the insurance placed on them hadn't been high, so nobody had paid much attention, especially as this was one bill Braceley had actually paid.

And where did they go?

They gave me the address of a warehouse on the outskirts of London.

And this time a night guard with a warehouse named Whittakers did his best to help and put me in touch with a very proper Englishman who was just finishing his dinner.

Speaking as if his mouth were stuffed with red-hot pebbles, the gentleman said he recalled the Seraphine shipment perfectly. After a mere two months Seraphine — who, he admitted, was unforgettable — had arrived with a hired van to remove the paintings. The van was not from any firm he'd ever heard of. No destination had been recorded. And the signature on the release sheet was totally illegible. The entire proceeding, he informed me, was highly irregular, which was why he remembered. But she *had* paid.

Where did he think the paintings had gone?

Probably hung them in her house, he replied disdainfully, as if that were the last place one would put pictures. Or, even worse, stored them in a garage. In any event, his records had showed that they were a bunch of unknowns, so who cared? Why the uproar over a collection of nobodies?

I asked him if they could have gone to another art warehouse and he snorted derisively. Not a prayer . . . any other warehouse, seeing the famous Whittakers label, would have called to ask the reason for the transfer, suspecting a deadbeat collector. I could waste my time checking further, he said, but it would be a true waste of time. I took him at his word and ended the search.

So Seraphine had sent a portion of her collection to England. She had either preceded or followed it there, married one or two or three people and then moved on.

And she had ended up in Amsterdam.

Had the paintings ended up there, too?

Chapter 23

The bouquet arrived the next morning.

It was lying on my doorstep when I stepped outside. There was no card — no indication of where it had been bought. Just a dozen red roses in a plastic wrapping.

I've heard it said that the only way to persuade a recalcitrant camel to rise to its feet and go to work is to light a fire under its derrière.

A dozen red roses did the trick for me.

I did an about-face and went back inside the house. The call I had to make was too important to be overheard by anyone at the gallery.

"Ed?" I didn't pause to ask how his institutional green walls were doing, which should have warned him. "There's a crisis here. I just received a bouquet of flowers."

Atlas weary of holding up the world couldn't have heaved a more heartfelt sigh. "Oh, it's you, Persis. Didn't you get the message I left on your machine? And since when is a bouquet of flowers a crisis in your life? I imagine you get flowers all the time."

"Not as often as you might think, I'm sorry to say. But these are roses, Ed — *roses*. A real emergency. And I think it has to do with the Body on the Power Mower."

This time he was really cross. "The *what?* Come on, Persis, I'm busy. I mean it."

"I know you're a federal employee, which probably means you're a slave, but if you have any influence with that firm you work for, I could use your help." Simms doesn't like it bandied about that he's FBI — he does a lot of undercover work — meeting crooks in dark parking lots to exchange monies and paintings and other such adventures: so he likes to keep a low profile.

But I'd finally piqued his interest. Or a premonition. "Influence for what kind of help?"

"Didn't I hear you say something about having to go to Paris on business?"

"That's right. You did."

"As I recall, you said you were having trouble trying to find the time. Could you possibly find the time tomorrow?"

That's one of the things that makes Ed Simms a great man: most of the time he's a stickler for regulations; and he can natter over details until you are ready to kill him.

to be my farewell gift to the Bureau."

"Your what?"

"Retiring — they're disbanding the Art Theft Squad. I've put in twenty years, so I'm eligible for retirement. It will be Simms Investigative Services after that."

It was the season for murders. Now it was the FBI Art Squad biting the dust.

"I'm sorry, Ed."

"Don't be. You're sure this trip is important, Persis?" His natural caution was reasserting itself.

"Never more so. It could actually be a matter of life and death."

"Whose?"

"Take your pick — there have already been three."

He didn't ask another question. All he said was, "Pack up. I'll pick you up tomorrow."

"I'll be waiting."

I hustled around the rest of the day trying to tie up loose ends.

It was evening before I was able to tie up the last loose end: the Amsterdam number hadn't answered all day long; all I got was a recording with the universal message, "We are not in at the moment, but if you will leave your name and number, we will get back to you as soon as possible." Answering machines all over the

But just when you think there's no hope, he displays the reckless derring-do and disregard for the system of a Captain Blood. Furthermore, there was the help I'd given him once in cracking a major art theft and he couldn't really refuse me.

"Possibly," he said.

"On the first flight out? Tourist class, of course."

"Naturally of course. Is there any other way? What could be more normal than to drop everything and rush off to Europe in the middle of the day tourist class?" He tried for a note of heavy sarcasm and succeeded brilliantly.

"You do your business — then we'll drive to Reims."

"Reims, is it? Well, I won't ask you why on the phone." Simms is convinced that all telephones are eternally bugged and that if they aren't they should be. "How about you? Can you get away?"

"Gregor will just have to do without me. I have my passport, visa, credit cards, and some cash. That's all you need to travel these days. Please, Ed. I'm serious."

"Well, I have to get the Paris thing over with some time. I've been promising Interpol for months to advise them on a projected art theft index they're setting up — it's going world were probably giving the same frustrating message to frustrated callers. This time I had to deliver my message personally.

About midnight Amsterdam time Mia finally answered.

"I'm leaving for Reims tomorrow," I told her. "But first there are things I want to ask you, and I think you will want to keep this conversation confidential."

"Meaning Frans, I suppose?"

"Actually meaning everyone. You see, I know that you were Sandro Corsini's first wife."

There was a hesitant laugh. "Well, I never made a secret of it, you know."

"But *he* did."

"Because I walked out on him — his ego couldn't stand it. I found he'd gotten the housekeeper pregnant, and like a fool I tried to kill myself. Then I thought I'd kill him. *Then* I thought — why? We Dutch are a practical people, after all. So I did the sensible thing and left him instead." Daniel Brodsk. Sandro Corsini's son.

"But now you're planning a show of Corsini in your gallery, aren't you?"

"Why not? Bygones are bygones and business is business."

This soft Dutch woman was tougher than she seemed. Maybe her marriage to Sandy had taught her. "Did you know that the representative he sent to make the arrangements was that same illegitimate son?"

For the first time there was a trace of emotion — just the slightest shock in her voice. "His son? Constanza's . . . ?" She didn't finish.

"I'm afraid so."

"But he was too old. His name was Broadman. He had gray hair. It couldn't be."

"It was. He handles everything for Sandy, who must have thought it was a big joke to have his illegitimate son, the reason you left, right there working with you . . . and neither one of you knowing who the other was."

"Of course. The Machiavellian, immoral bastard."

"And when exactly was he there?"

She thought. "Several times. But I am too upset to remember. His son! It couldn't have been. The son would only be twenty-two or -three years old."

"I'm afraid he was. The gray hair — Sandy would think it a great laugh. A sort of childish revenge for leaving him. I'm sorry."

"That is why you called?"

"That, and to tell you to be careful. Also, will you tell me if Sandy painted you — and if he did — how?"

But the Dutch art dealer had had enough.

"That is none of your affair, Mrs. Willum." She must have envisioned her chances for a Gainsborough Brown show flying out the window and she must not have cared, because she hung up on me. And I could imagine a dozen reasons why.

Chapter 24

You could never accuse Ed Simms of being a nosy man. Once on the airplane he asked me ten succinct questions, mulled over my answers, asked about ten more equally succinct questions, and lapsed into a deep and thoughtful silence from which he roused himself only to toy with the dreary airline meal — Simms is a notorious gourmet — and read his *International Herald Tribune*.

On the autoroute to Reims he wasn't much better — he talked mainly about how they were disbanding the Art Squad and about how all cases would be turned over to a single agent in Chicago who would handle them in addition to his regular caseload. Simms's life was art: the ending of the squad was equal to the ending of his life. I knew he'd like to make one final hurrah before retirement.

Which was why we were here together.

It wasn't a long trip from Paris. His rendezvous with Interpol had actually taken up most of the day but we'd be in Reims in time for dinner and a good night's sleep.

"I'm going to treat you to a decent meal," he told me as we pulled up to the Hotel Bristol on the Place Drouet d'Erlon. "This is a modest hotel without a restaurant, so what we lose on the Ferris wheel we'll make up on the merry-go-round . . . we can afford dinner at G. and J. Benoit . . . that's Georges and Jacques, two old friends."

I wasn't sure I was up to a real French meal: my nerves were frayed and so was my stomach. The bouquet of roses had done it.

"I'm not hungry . . ."

"Don't be silly. I'm here to look after you, aren't I? Besides, we have to celebrate my imminent divorce after my twenty-year marriage to the Bureau. Don't people always celebrate their divorces?"

"I've never had one." Pure chance — if I hadn't been a widow first, I'd certainly have been a divorcee.

He was already ushering me into Le Chardonnay and the hosts were rushing out to pump Simms's hand, followed by the chef in his towering toque. A passionate discussion among the four men ensued before everyone was satisfied and the chef consented to return to his kitchen.

"They've decided to give us truffe en croûte,

filet de bar à la julienne de légumes, and boeuf au Bouzy et à la Moëlle followed by the great house dessert, a délice de Marjorie." Simms spoke not one word of French, but he could make his way through a French menu like a knife through melting butter.

It was one of the many contradictions about Ed Simms that I will never understand.

"Another last supper," I mumbled glumly, my war-torn stomach recoiling.

"Don't be absurd. You'll love it."

And he was right: I did.

When the last drop of Perrier-Jouët with which we'd celebrated the meal was gone, we prepared to stagger out of the restaurant.

"I will never eat again," I declared.

"We have to buy a local map somewhere for tomorrow," he reminded me.

"I thought you did that before we left home?"

"Couldn't get a detailed one. Have to find a brasserie somewhere. Tell you what: I'll take the car for this search and maybe you'd like to walk off the dinner by footing it back to the hotel?"

Nothing would suit me better. "I'll never make it through tomorrow if I don't."

"Off you go, then, while I settle the bill. See you back at the hotel in a few minutes."

But it was longer than that before one of

the Benoits came with the police. I think the Benoit was Georges, but I'm not sure.

He took my hand. His eyes were sad.

"It's bad news, I'm afraid."

The police nodded agreement. Their eyes were also sad.

"It's Monsieur Simms. The car — it blew up. We have had labor troubles at Le Chardonnay. Most regrettable. We have a guard. But he was drunk, you know."

I was missing something — something important. "A car blew up? *Our* car?"

They all shook their heads and looked devastated.

"Regrettably. So sorry."

"And Simms? You're telling me . . . ?"

"That he was in it. We are so sorry."

Simms! And I was supposed to have been in it, too.

"He's . . . ?"

"So sorry. We were all there instantly — it was in the parking lot of the restaurant. But too late. Nothing we could do. So very sorry."

There was more, I suppose. Probably lots more. But I don't remember it. Because all the time I was thinking, it's my fault — I talked him into coming. He was there because of me. He got into that car because of me. Because he trusted me, because he *believed* me.

And because he wanted his last hurrah.

"I owe you one, Simms," I said to myself. "You can count on me."

I hoped it was true, but I was far from sure. After all, I hadn't planned to have to count only on myself.

Chapter 25

I thought dawn would never arrive. But just when I'd given up all hope, it did. Not rosy-fingered and full of promise the way it's supposed to, but pale and wan and sickly as a vow of eternal love that would never be kept.

After two cups of coffee, I dressed hurriedly, leased a new car, and drove down the street to the first brasserie that carried maps of the region. It was about noon when I finally left Reims behind and entered the Ardennes, driving along miles of straight, deserted highway that dipped almost imperceptibly up and down toward a horizon unencumbered by buildings or signs of life other than the occasional lonely piece of medieval-looking farm equipment.

The deeper I penetrated into the Ardennes, the more poverty-stricken and deserted it looked. Falling-down barns, hovels for homes. Hopeless hamlets with three or four houses leaning on one another for support. Piles of brick and lumber where buildings had collapsed from neglect.

Even the occasional larger village along the route had such an air of despair that no traveler would be tempted to stop to ask directions.

My detailed map showed that the village I was looking for did exist, although judging from the size of the type it existed but barely and at the end of a spidery tangle of lines that indicated little more than cart tracks. Still, it was on the map: I hadn't been dreaming. And that was a comfort. Simms would have been pleased with me.

According to the map, the two nearest cities were Reims, which I'd just quitted, and Laon, the walled capital of the region in the times of Charlemagne, birthplace of his mother, the marvelously named Bertha Bigfoot.

By noon the road was empty with the exception of a fugitive tractor crawling from the endless, rolling fields to some unseen home for lunch. The landscape was like a deserted planet, bereft of life. Unenthusiastic fields of different colored crops, mostly dusty burnt siennas, created a dull patchwork of squares. Now and then a lone cow appeared, grazing dispiritedly in a field barren of trees. Once I saw a troop of young bulls, huddled together against the flies, ears stapled with orange labels and twitching listlessly.

Another time I noted a flock of sheep. They had large red numbers painted on their backs.

The few houses I saw were miles apart and usually so far off the road that I wondered if they had been built in the old days to hide from the invading Wehrmacht. Once or twice I saw the spires of churches, hidden in the valleys.

It was about one-thirty. After endless pauses at the side of the road to consult my map, I had arrived at a moderately substantial-looking village called Montcornet. Either it was entirely deserted, or the good citizens were still celebrating the sacred lunch hour, because everything was closed up tight. The only sign of life was six red faces staring at me from the window of a café.

Before I could even get out of my car, the fiercely mustached barkeep anticipated my intention and barred the door with his body. No mere woman would intrude on this sacred male territory.

I explained that I was looking for a certain village. A flood of instruction burst from inside the bar, redolent with right turns, left turns, straight aheads, and direction this town, direction that. I could take my pick; but no two directions were alike.

Score one for you, Seraphine, I thought. Even the locals can't decide.

I thanked them and retreated to my car. The sound of furious debate followed me down the street as I drove away. Once out of town, I pulled over and studied the map again. I couldn't be too far away. Here was Montcornet — here were the squiggly lines, crossing one another, shooting off every which way. If I left the highway here . . . if I crossed this lane there . . .

So I did.

And there, finally, was a rusted sign that said "Rubigny."

If there were fifty souls in Rubigny, including rabbits, dogs, cats, and pigeons, it would be a miracle.

Altogether there weren't more than fifteen houses, barns, and rabbit pens. Most were clustered on two sides of a road that wound through a shallow valley and across a stream no wider than a single thread of silk. Many of the buildings were deserted — a mixed bag of styles: timbered daub and wattle, cement, gray slate, and red brick, often all in a single building. Many houses were attached to skeletons of barns with open sky peering through the timbers of the roofs. A square brick church like a fortress stood guard over this dismal array, a single, truncated spire rising bravely from its prow. In front of the church, a World

War I soldier cast in cement and painted brown lounged against a cement post, his hands crossed contentedly on his stomach. The names of the village dead of both World Wars and Algeria were carved in the stone below. It was a short list.

I heard the hoarse barking of a chained-up dog somewhere and I saw a cow foraging knee-deep in the mud of a front yard.

Except for one lone man in workman's blue washing down his car there were no people in sight. It was still lunchtime.

I decided to make a double tour of Rubigny's single road. Down to the stream, where there was a monument to three dead FFI resistance fighters of World War II. Back to the top and the foraging cow. Back again.

The village tour didn't take two minutes.

Then I stepped on my brakes.

The house looked, at first glance, like any other — slightly run-down and with the usual attached barn, daylight streaming through the timbers of the fallen roof.

But the hardware — the shutters . . . they were new. I pulled out my sketchbook and began to draw furiously. If anyone was watching I was just a touring artist.

The side that formed the angle with the barn had once been Normandy-style timbered daub and wattle. There were two shuttered windows and a shuttered door. The other sides of the house were without any windows, the only light into the interior being small square openings here and there in the walls. Obviously the peasant farmers preferred warmth to light. They went to bed with the birds, anyway.

The door was also new.

I jumped out of the car and moved around the far side of this seemingly falling-down wreck.

And I saw what I expected to see: on the other three sides of the house the frames of the small openings had been recently reinforced and the glass beneath the smeared dirt and mud was new and shiny.

I kept on sketching, in case anyone was looking. It was like automatic writing. I let my pencil work while I sorted out my thoughts.

Of course. The very last place anyone like Seraphine would have chosen. Rubigny, the most lost of lost villages.

I toured the house again, studying the small apertures. None was larger than twenty-four-by-thirty-six inches. I picked up a stick from the ground and, using it as a ruler, measured the largest opening. Then I measured myself. I'm small. Small hips. Small bosom. It might just work.

I picked up a rock, wrapping it in my jacket to muffle the sound, and, standing on a bench covered with empty flowerpots, I broke the largest opening, careful to leave no jagged edges, with as little noise as possible. It took only a few seconds and made hardly a sound.

There was one minute when I thought I'd be stuck forever, wriggling hopelessly. Then a final desperate wriggle and the bottleneck broke. I tumbled with a bruising thump onto a hard stone floor.

The small flashlight I always carry in my bag crept timorously over the rough stone walls of the interior — the closed shutters made it very dark inside — until it found a light switch. I touched it and the darkness vanished. Another modern improvement.

Great dark timbers crossed the ceiling. One wall held a stone sink, the other a smoke-stained brick fireplace with a curved bread oven built into its side. The old stone floor was cold and damp beneath my feet.

There was a minimum of furniture — coarse country stuff that no self-respecting thief would deign to steal. No rug. A few plates and cups standing on the mantel.

Nothing else.

Two doors led off this barren room.

The first opened onto what was obviously a bedroom. The furnishings were sparse — just a mattress on a wooden frame and a dressing table with a simple array of cosmetics. Frosted sliding doors separated this room from a modern bathroom. There were no clothes; nothing to betray the owner of this house.

The second door was something else. It opened into a room the size of the bedroom, very dark behind its closed and locked outside shutters.

But there was a light switch on the wall. I flicked it on.

I was standing in a storeroom. And it was full of wrapped-up paintings. There must have been forty.

Simms, I thought, if only you were here. I think we've found your last hurrah, the cache of your lifetime.

Chapter 26

It took forever, but I was determined not to hurry. I owed it to Seraphine — I owed it to Simms — to do this right.

With the utmost care, I undressed the paintings. One by one I removed the wrappings, noting down the codes on their coverings in my sketchbook and repeating the same information on their backs.

And slowly, carefully, they all emerged.

First came Mia and Constanza Brodsk, their nude, ivory-white bodies close together behind the bathing screen that hid them from the waist down. Each was wearing an earring, but nothing else. One was blond, the other brunette, and they stared impassively out of the canvas as if to say, "Well, didn't you guess after all this time?"

Each was self-consciously half smiling; and the thumb and forefinger of Mia's left hand were delicately touching the rosy tip of Constanza's marble-white bosom as if to show off its beauty.

The signature in the lower right read: "Sandro Corsini after an Anonymous French Master's portrait of the beautiful Gabrielle and the Maréchale de Balagny."

Anonymous French Master — Mia, Constanza.

I knew the original well. It is one of the great treasures of the Louvre, an example of the kind of portrait painting that was popular in French court circles during the sixteenth century, portraits that were sent as gifts for weddings and other special occasions. It is believed that this particular painting, showing Gabrielle taking a bath with her sister, was done to celebrate the fertility of Gabrielle d'Estree, pregnant by King Henry IV, who was preparing to divorce Margaret of Valois to marry his mistress when she died in childbirth in 1599.

And Sandy had painted this version to celebrate the pregnancy of his housekeeper-mistress and humiliate his wife.

AFM-MC. That much of the code was now clear. And the numbers? The final four of Mia's telephone exchange. I should know — I'd just called it two days ago.

I continued to unwrap the paintings, so involved in my work that a flight of Mirage jets hurling themselves directly into the building wouldn't have startled me.

And gradually they all emerged — all the ladies of Gull Harbor. All beautifully, proudly, amorously, totally naked. All unmistakably recognizable.

And all of them starring as the centerpiece of Sandy's tribute to some great painter.

Sam Swann lying deliciously nude in the middle of a forest on a blue robe, one arm flung behind her head, hair in disarray, waiting for the lover who leans over her. Corsini after Correggio's *Antiope,* first in the series representing the loves of Jupiter. C-SS.

Angela Roth with pearls in her hair and nothing else except her own golden skin. Corsini after François Boucher's *Diana Resting.* FB-AR.

Tinka Wheeler in bracelets and strings of beads and a lustful gaze as one of the figures in a Turkish harem after Jean Auguste Dominique Ingre's *The Turkish Bath.*

Betsy Smith with pendulous breasts and riotous thighs as a writhing Peter Paul Rubens nude from *The Arrival of Marie de Medici at Marseilles.*

Marianna McCoy caught unglamorously naked, disheveled, and unaware in her bath, looking as if Degas and Sandy had painted her while looking through a keyhole.

Christine Kelley very ugly as Georges Seurat's knobby pointillist *The Model,* nude but scarcely flattered by the artist.

Missy Braceley — the "innocent" debutante — overeager on a rumpled bed as Jean-Honoré Fragonard's *La Chemise Enlevée*.

And Seraphine — always Seraphine.

All the pillars of Gull Harbor society. And not once, but over and over again in "tributes," to all the great painters — Gauguin, Courbet, Picasso, Mantegna, Matisse, Goya, Giorgione, Grünewald, Cranach, Rembrandt, Botticelli, Delacroix, Eakins, Blake, Modigliani. And all of them languorous, amorous, and naked as the day they were born.

Marianna McCoy. Missy Braceley. Betsy Smith. Angela Roth, Tinka Wheeler. Sam Swann. Christine Kelley. Names that made the society columns quake. Husbands that ruled financial worlds.

And there was more — portfolios full of working sketches of the illustrious society matrons sprawled on the animal skin of Sandy's famous studio bed, their eyes heavy with amour. Sketches in pencil, silverpoint, charcoal, conté crayon, ink and brush. Women who had just made love, and not with their husbands.

All clearly recognizable sketches of interludes of dalliance before the paintings to come.

I understood everything all too clearly: Sandy had followed in the tradition of artists of the past.

The great Goya's delicious *Nude Maja* and Manet's *Olympia* had probably been inspired by such masterpieces as Titian's *Venus of Urbino*, in which the duchess of Urbino had posed for the head and a curvaceous courtesan for the nude body, to the evident satisfaction of both. And before that there was Giorgione's sensuous *Sleeping Venus*, the ideal nude of every man's and every artist's dreams.

To pay tribute to the painters who celebrated the nude was traditional in art. It was even traditional to use high-born women as models — the duchess of Urbino, for example, and Goya's duchess of Alba.

But a whole community of famous women? With famous husbands? In prudish America? Let alone in stuffy Gull Harbor?

Just like Sandy, I suppose. He couldn't resist leaving proof that he had had them all in his bed.

"That devil," I said out loud.

"I couldn't agree more — he is every inch of that. And thanks for riding point."

He was standing in the doorway. I didn't have to ask his intentions — the gun he held was directed straight at me.

"Don't you know every neighbor has a key

in France?" he continued politely, dryly. "You could have entered with me through the front door instead of crawling through a hole in the wall. Well, we'll leave together like civilized people."

"No —"

"I've put your car in the barn. If anyone notices or cares they'll think it's hers." His tone was so everyday you might have thought he was bored; that he didn't believe the situation himself. But the gun disproved it.

"Simms knows I'm here," I said.

"Simms is dead. So don't make a fuss."

"How did you follow . . . there wasn't a car in sight . . . I was watching."

He had my arm now. "Basic electronics. A small device, that's all. Placed while you were in buying your map at the brasserie."

"Someone . . . Gregor . . ."

"They'll find you lying beside one of these God-forsaken roads. The roses are in the car. It's the last *beau geste* in the Messenger's tradition."

"The last *beau geste?* On the contrary," said the new voice I never thought I'd hear again, "I would say it was the last hurrah."

Neither one of us had noticed; we were too busy playing out our little drama.

Jordan Braceley's reflexes were good, but

not quite good enough. He fired as he whirled, but his shot went wide. Ed Simms's bullet reached him first.

"I never thought I'd finish my career in a blaze of gunfire." Regret was written all over Simms's square, scrubbed, all-American face. "But we couldn't lose you in an unhappy ending, could we?"

"Well, at least he was sending me roses," I said. "I don't get that many bouquets."

"I'll send you a trainload tomorrow to help you forget."

And he did.

Chapter 27

The room was full of flowers. Roses. Red roses.

"Tears came to the eyes of even the holy gods," I said.

Gregor was not pleased. It was the flowers. He was not pleased because he himself had not sent them. Also he was allergic. "What are you mumbling about, Persis? I don't understand what you're saying."

I sighed. "It's nothing, Gregor. I was thinking of Seraphine and quoting Sappho. Sappho had an appreciation for beautiful women: she would have loved Seraphine. That's all."

"Oh." He sneezed and wiped his nose and glared at Ed Simms, who was seated across the room, a halo of red roses behind his head, stroking Isadore Duncan, who had fallen in love with him on sight and was now lying on her back across his knees, purring rhythmically and regarding him through half-closed, love-crazed eyes.

The original two police were there, too.

"It's Henrietta's fault," I told them. Not that they were going to believe me — I could see that at once. "If it hadn't been for her mania for social respectability, none of it would have happened. Seraphine would be alive, and everyone else."

"Open the door, will you?" Gregor sneezed some more. "I can't breathe with all these damn roses around. I didn't think roses were proper for funeral flowers."

One of the detectives complied.

"You've missed the point," Simms said, unperturbed. "The roses are for Persis. A personal tribute."

Gregor was annoyed. "So what about Henrietta?"

It wasn't going to be easy; but it had to be done.

"Seraphine believed every word her mother ever said. And my theory is that when she married Dehorter and found out there wasn't any rainbow at the end of the marriage ceremony, that there wasn't in fact even any sex, she fell easily into the clutches of the amorously immoral Corsini. He was the other extreme. And then when she discovered all those painted documentations of his faithlessness, she went quite crazy. She stole the paintings, embarked on her famous life of sin, and began to blackmail all the ladies in

Sandy's life, ladies who would pay anything to keep their husbands from knowing they'd been frolicking in Sandy's bed."

"Hah!" said Gregor. "I might have guessed."

The two detectives, names still unsorted in my mind, were enthralled. "But there was a limit, wasn't there?" they asked.

"Indeed there was, even for them. And when they reached it . . ." I looked to Ed Simms for help.

"Seraphine, who hadn't received a dime from either of her first two husbands, threatened to sell the exhibition and photographs of the paintings to *Life* or *Penthouse* or *Playboy*. She actually went so far as to get a good offer, armed with which she approached the stunned husbands of the ladies involved."

"My God." Out came Gregor's famous white handkerchief. The brow-mopping began.

"So all of them wanted to do away with her, I suppose," said one of the upholders of the law.

"Quite so. But it took the formidable Henrietta Braceley to get it done — in her own unique way." Simms shook his head disapprovingly. "Remarkable woman."

"It was the family honor. Even Missy's name was involved — the final blow, you might say. You'd have to know Henrietta ... But of course you do, don't you, Gregor? She couldn't have more scandal — not after the *Olympia* lawsuit and everything. It was the last straw as far as she was concerned. Seraphine had gone one step too far. Henrietta told Jordan he had to do something. I don't suppose she actually meant murder. But he had to obey his mother; and in the end it was all he could think of — Seraphine wouldn't listen to reason."

Gregor gasped and reached for a magazine to fan himself. It was, naturally, *Town and Country*. "I think I may die," he whispered.

Simms rose immediately and opened a window.

"Don't worry," I said. "It's a temporary weakness." I turned to Gregor. "You know what's coming, don't you?"

"I think so." He was very pale. "Jordan Braceley was the last one, wasn't he? She said 'you have to do something — your wife ... the children ... save the family honor.' So he did."

Gregor was right. There were too many roses in the room. There wasn't any air at all. But still, it was magnificent in a decadent sort of way. Fitting, you might say. "He had to do something. You know Henrietta — you know he *had* to."

The two policemen were wide-eyed. Ed Simms looked pained.

"He went to that poor young fool Brodsk, didn't he?"

Simms did the honors. "Brodsk was the messenger . . . the classic ill-fated messenger. Jordan persuaded him that his mother's reputation was at stake — his father's, too. And after such a scandal he'd never have a chance in Gull Harbor society — he had great hopes, you know. The ladies had been giving him quite a rush. Murder wasn't Jordan's style; but Brodsk was perfect. It was easy for Jordan to arrange all the business at Harrington House — Brodsk was never there, of course."

"He was going to Amsterdam anyway to arrange Sandy's show," I put in. "Seraphine didn't recognize him — how could she? He was about fifteen when she left. But he was attractive. And willing. Still, she must have sensed something. So she arranged to put the painting on the Air France flight. Before the plane took off there was plenty of time to lure her back to the car. He gave her flowers to thank her for the night she'd given him. Then he killed her. It wasn't the first time, you see. He wasn't a neophyte."

"The Famous Correspondent?" Gregor asked.

"He caught her trying to photograph the *Olympia*. I don't suppose he meant to kill her. But it happened. He was just a kid. And Sandy had said something like 'don't let anyone see this painting until I give the word. Guard it with your life.' Sandy's orders were sacred."

"Seraphine was one thing," Simms said. "He had no love for her: she'd once moved into the position he thought belonged to his mother. And he believed she was threatening everyone in Gull Harbor. So he killed her — destroyed her famous notebook. But when it came to you . . . when Braceley decided you were getting too close . . . Brodsk couldn't do it. He liked you. You'd always been kind. He just couldn't do it. He was a mixed-up, psychotic kid — and no wonder, living with a father who wouldn't acknowledge him. But he drew the line at hurting you."

"He sent me roses. They came the day after he died."

"So Braceley killed him, and set out to dispose of you himself. By then he had no other way out."

Isadore had managed to rise from Simms's lap and was draped around his neck, rallying now and then to kiss his cheek. It was a shocking display. "You knew it all along, didn't you?" I asked Simms.

"Well, more or less."

"You arranged your own demise."

"With a little help from the Boyers and the French police. It was easy enough. And what's one car more or less where three murders are involved? It was important that Braceley believed you were alone."

"You were the man washing the car. Poor Braceley. Murder wasn't his kind of thing — but he thought it was his duty. He didn't do it very well."

"Henrietta would say he failed the family," Gregor mused.

"It was Henrietta's fault," I said once more. "All of it, from the beginning. But I don't suppose she'll ever admit it. It's so sad, really. . . . She ruined Seraphine and Seraphine ruined everything else."

"Exactly," they agreed.

"Seraphine deserved better."

"Absolutely," they agreed again.

"No girl who ever was

O groom, was like her."

"Meaning what?" they asked.

"Meaning nothing, really. Sappho again. A song for Seraphine, I guess."

It was the least I could say, the least I could do, under the circumstances.

It was the nearest I could come to an alibi for Seraphine, who needed one because she, alas, was too beautiful.